Lady of the Court:
Book Two of The Three Graces Trilogy

Laura du Pre

Table of Contents

Henriette, Paris, 1573

I have to hand it to Claude Catherine; she's managed to pull off quite a gathering tonight. Anyone who is anyone in Paris is packed into her salon, making it much warmer than the crisp October air outside. I slipped outside to take a break a few minutes earlier and by the time I returned, the festivities were in full swing. On this particular night, Claude invited painters, poets, sculptors, writers, everyone in Paris with an artistic bent, and in the midst of everything Margot, Queen of Navarre holds court.

"Madame de Nevers," an undistinguishable woman whose name I cannot place nods at me, a trail of perfume following behind her. This may not be my party, but even the outliers of the court know that I am a force to be reckoned with. They say that I am the richest woman in France; and I would not deny that fact. My wealth was not simply handed to me, I worked hard for every crown and every sou that I possess. Unlike most people at court, if I lost my entire fortune in an instant, I could build it back up with my own efforts. That is what they fear most about me. I rely on no one, not even the King himself.

I stand behind one of the elegant chairs Claude's servants pushed in from the ballroom and glance at the actor standing in front of the crowd. As the Duchess de Retz, she has the money and taste to afford the furnishings that make her Hotel the envy of Paris. I pause for a moment to admire her décor, something that she constantly threatens to tear down and replace with something new. Within a few seconds, I look in Margot's direction. She's bored, but does her best to give the impression that the man has not bored her sleep. Few people would suspect that she is anything less than enraptured with his performance.

"God, he's terrible." A male voice slices into my ear and I turn to stare at him. I agree with him, but I don't appreciate the intrusion on my thoughts or my personal space.

Turning, I get a good look at him and lift one expertly plucked eyebrow. The motion never fails to intimidate a man foolhardy enough to try to go head to head with me. I enjoy the challenge of a good conversation and I want to know if the interloper is up to the task.

"You're an expert on actors, then?"

"Madame, I'm an expert on men, and this one can't muster up an authentic emotion to save his life." This was proving to be promising. He could keep up with me so far. I pressed further.

"Then, I suppose you're available to instruct someone on the finer points of acting?"

He gave me an elegant nod, "Madame, I am prepared to give you instruction, any time you wish. He wiggles his eyebrows suggestively. It would seem, however, that the man standing in front of us needs my help more than you do." A good save, flirtatious, the invitation open. He was a bold one. I was about to respond when the performance blessedly ended and a round of polite applause erupted.

"Henriette, sit with me. We're about to have a song!" Margot could barely speak through her giggles. A second later and she had collapsed into them. "Excuse me, Monsieur," I rushed past him to see what had Margot all atwitter. I was disappointed that I could not spar with him any further, but given his performance so far, I was sure that I'd see him again soon.

"Aloysius, you must give us one of your poems tonight!" Margot pulled me next to her and threw her feathered fan to hide her face. "Help me, that actor was terrible! We have to do something or the night is in jeopardy."

She pulled her fan down, her mask of gaiety back. Margot knew better than any thespian in France the benefit of showing an external face. *She could teach acting,* I thought to myself. The thought of Margot Valois, Queen of Navarre starting an acting troupe made me laugh almost as loudly as she had done a few moments earlier. A second thought followed, the realization that knowing Margot, starting a troupe of actors was exactly the kind of outrageous thing she would do. That particular thought had me in hysterics and I could not stop myself. Margot turned to me and pulled a face.

"What on earth is wrong with you? It wasn't that funny!"

I turned towards Margot and covered my mouth with my hand. "I'll tell you later. Aloysius, get up here now!" I gave him my most imperious look and he bounded to his feet in seconds. Some men were so easy to intimidate.

I spent the rest of the evening at Margot's side, both of us determined to keep the actor from ruining the evening by returning to the makeshift stage in front of Claude's massive fireplace. Since her marriage, Margot was determined to enjoy every moment of Parisian society she had left until she was packed off to the countryside to rule Navarre with her husband. I could barely blame her, given what I had heard about Navarre from my own sister Marie. Apparently, the entire county thrived on misery and boredom. Navarre had converted to Protestantism, a strict flavor of heresy that encouraged a lifetime of dour behavior and sour faces. With their stark black clothing and stripped down worship services, these men and women took everything enjoyable out of a religious service. Not only were their services dull, they were downright depressing. I shuddered at the thought of having to sit through one of them.

Thank God Marie was safe in Paris and away from the influence of the Protestants. Our Aunt Jeanne would have dragged us all into damnation with her heresy if given the chance. Margot had her work cut out for her, presiding over those humorless followers of John Calvin and his teachings. Most people would be intimidated by the idea of presiding over a court that did not want them, but Margot was not the kind of woman to be intimidated by the simple fact that she was not wanted.

I found Margot the following afternoon in her privy chamber, lying on a divan, reading. She moved her lower legs to allow me to sit next to her. "Were you distracted last night at Claude's salon? Because I felt like you were distracted."

That was Margot, blunt when she wanted to be; and always perceptive. Many people saw her beauty and her glamorous facade, and assumed that she would be stupid, but they were quickly disappointed to find out that she was quite the opposite. Margot never failed to notice anything.

"I was having a conversation before I sat down with you and I was still thinking about it." I hoped that this small lie was close enough to the truth to satisfy her curiosity.

"About what?" She snapped the book closed.

"About starting an acting troupe here in Paris."

She snorted, "As if I had time for something like that. You had an entire conversation about an acting troupe? That sounds suspicious."

Margot then fell silent. She could wait me out until I confessed. She had managed to do just that to me so many times before that I knew it was useless to try and outsmart her. She might be a decade younger than I, but she could outmaneuver anyone.

"It wasn't the topic, it was the tone of the conversation." I sighed, giving unto her insatiable curiosity.

"The tone of the person speaking?" She was splitting hairs, trying to get at the truth.

I threw my hands in the air, "Were you watching me?" She bit her lip like a naughty girl. I had thought that she was engrossed in her own conversation, but apparently, she never missed anything.

"I saw you talking with a man and it looked animated. So," she tapped her fingers on the book lightly, drawing me in, "who was he?"

"You don't even know? There are men at the court that you do not know?"

She shook her head, enjoying my discomfort. "No, wait—maybe I do. He's someone in my brother's household. Now, what was his name?" The tapping continued as she played with me like a cat and a mouse. "He's from Gascony and he has some tropical sounding name."

"Coconnas." I was getting tired of her teasing.

Sensing that I was tired of the game, she changed her tone. "Sorry, but as long as I've known you, you have never bothered to take a lover. That's," she waved her hands in the air dramatically, "a little odd for someone in your place. Were I as rich as you, I'd have a line of lovers waiting outside my door."

"Are you saying that I'm boring?" I looked at her with mock horror, which sent her into a fit of giggles. Margot was always up for a bit of fun.

"Yes, whoever heard of a woman who loved and was faithful to her husband?" She shuddered with mock horror.

"I've been quite pleased with Louis, thank you. He's never caused me a moment of trouble and I don't have any plans to cause him a moment of trouble, either."

"But you did find Coconnas attractive?'

"Margot, I'm married, not a corpse." I gave her a thin smile, conceding her point.

I returned home to the Hotel de Nevers, our Paris home, late that evening. Louis met me at the top of the stairs to our bedchamber. "He's not much better," the corners of his eyes creased and I saw dark bags under his eyes.

I let out a long sigh. "Did the physician say anything about why he's losing so much weight?'

My husband shook his head, "He thinks that it is a malignant tumor, or perhaps something in his blood. Without healthy blood, there can be no vigor."

A better mother would have rushed to her child's bedside to soothe her son. A better mother would know what to say to the boy who wasted away in front of our eyes. A better mother would not spend hours away from her own home because she could not stand the feelings of guilt and helplessness that came with caring for an ailing child. Since my son only had me for a mother, I hid at the Louvre for hours on end to keep from facing the apprehension that cast a dark cloud over our home.

"He's asleep; I would let him rest until tomorrow morning." Louis gently touched my shoulder and I placed my hand on his. None of my money or his favor with the king could help us in this situation. We were simply two grieving parents who stood by and begged God to show us mercy. So far, God had decided not to do so, but we still held out hope that one day he would change his mind. Louis headed back to his study and I drifted to my bedchamber like a wraith.

Frederick was our only son and he had not even made it to his first birthday. When he came into the world, this past spring, he was pink and gave a lusty cry. Getting a child past the dangers of childbirth was dangerous enough and when we both survived the ordeal, I had thought that he had survived the worst. At four months, when his older sisters began to put on pounds and become fat cheeked cherubs, our son instead became thin and gaunt. We tried every remedy we could think of and consulted the midwives and wet nurses of Paris, but nothing worked. Soon the doctors began to arrive, including the most well-respected surgeons from Italy. Even they could not tell us for certain what was wrong with our son or whether he would survive.

We had two consolations that kept us from falling into total despair, our daughters Catherine, an opinionated girl of five and her sister, Marie who was all of two years old. Unlike her sister, Marie barely gave us any trouble as she was an obedient and quiet girl much like her father. While our daughters were proving to be quite healthy, we could not say the same for our only son.

Margot loves to tease me about my methodical nature, a quality that thankfully my husband shares. We both thought that once we noticed a problem with our child if we attacked it hard enough we would eventually find a solution for it. Our inability to find any relief for his suffering, has tried our faith in our own intellect.

Before, we could find solace in our shared ability to use reason, something that sustained our marriage for the past eight years. Louis and I have been very pleased with one another and along with our daughters, we formed quite a team. These days, however, my husband and I pass one another like specters. Faith and reason have deserted us, and I think that we have forgotten how to manage the simplest communications with one another.

The noise and frivolity of the court somehow managed to distract me and each day I welcomed the opportunity to escape. While Louis and I engaged in strained pleasantries, the court at large was a haven for pointless and spiteful gossip. It's the perfect place to raise your spirits with its shallow pursuits. This is why I welcomed the opportunity to sit and watch a tennis game one mild afternoon in October.

"God help me, this is boring!" Charlotte de Sauve, wife of the Chancellor and the mistress of Margot's husband, the King of Navarre, rolled her eyes. Although her own lover was one of the players, she frequently sighed as if she might well die of the boredom.

Navarre dropped the ball and it rolled into the corner faster than he could run after it. "You stupid little beast!" Navarre ran after it, stumbling gracelessly as he did so. Navarre is my first cousin, although given how ungainly he is, you would not assume that we shared any family ties. Stories abound that he spent his first eight years living in a mud hut and eating insects at his grandfather's insistence. Given how bad he smells, I think there may be some truth in that rumor. Charlotte de Sauve must be truly desperate to spend any time in his bed, but given the fact that she does so at the Queen Mother's behest, I'm sure that she's paid quite well to do so.

"Baroness de Sauve, perhaps you would be happier going inside?" Margot turned to look at her husband's mistress and arched an eyebrow. Margot has no ill feelings toward Charlotte, due in part to the fact that Margot has no hesitation in taking lovers of her own. Neither of them came into their marriage as innocent babes, or as virgins. They have an implicit agreement that each is free to take lovers. It's an agreement that most royal brides would envy and Margot enjoys the freedom it gives her.

"No, it's best that I stay," Charlotte shot a wary glance at Catherine de Medici, who would no doubt berate her spy for failing to keep tabs on her assignment. No one could afford to anger the Queen Mother, especially someone as vulnerable as Madame de Sauve. Her husband rose under the Queen's patronage and she is dependent on the King's wishes to succeed her father as Vicomte de Tours.

I was once in Charlotte's place; eight years earlier, my brother James died and there were no brothers left to inherit my father's fortune. King Henry allowed me to become the Duchess of Nevers, but on the condition that I marry my second cousin, Louis and allow him to become the Duke of Nevers. Louis's mother was a

Frenchwoman and came with the Queen Mother in her Italian retinue. Upon Louis' grandmother's death, the King allowed him to inherit his grandmother's estates. In France, a woman could inherit, as long as it suited the King's needs in order to do so. As long as Charlotte plays Catherine's game and willingly supplies her with valuable information, she will inherit as I did. The trick is in pleasing the Valois and not angering them too much; and remaining useful to them.

Navarre's opponent in the game was my striking brother-in-law, the current Duc de Guise. Duke Henri stood about a head taller than the rest of the court, towering above even the very average looking Valois princes. Guise's flowing blond hair and his rough good looks broke quite a few hearts in the court, not the least of which was Margot's. The two came dangerously close to marrying until the Queen Mother wrenched them apart. The result of that wrenching was that Guise quickly married my sister, Catherine in a wedding that raised every eyebrow in Paris.

Although Catherine sat only a few seats away from me, we could not even lock eyes. The Guise were hemorrhaging money; and rather than face their creditors, they were determined to cover up that fact by demanding that Catherine get more than her share of our father's estate. I refused to be bullied by a family of spendthrifts, so I refused to give Catherine a sou more than she was due. As a result, she refuses to speak to me.

"Navarre, if it's too much for you, you can simply call the game!" Guise gives him a courtly bow, which would seem chivalrous, if we did not know how much Guise despised Navarre. He hid his dislike of my cousin as well as he hid his financial situation. I'm sure that Guise is putting Catherine up to this and I blame him for the greedy behavior more than I blame her. Catherine's passions have always swung from mood to mood and these days, she is more unpredictable than ever. She is due to give birth to their most recent child in December and within a few days, she will travel to Joinville to give birth. Knowing how easy it is to lose a child, I feel guilty that I am being unkind to her. I could possibly lose my sister in childbirth and the thought upsets me so that tears sting in my eyes. "Excuse me, I need to leave."   I trip over two of the Queen Mother's teenage demoiselles as I stumble from the court and into the palace.

Headed for a quieter place and one that is far away from my pregnant sister, I entered the Queen's presence chamber. The current Queen is a quiet and unassuming Austrian named Elisabeth, who unlike the rest of the court prefers to stay out of sight. I found the Queen and my youngest sister, Marie, stitching altar cloths.
"What did we miss?" Marie held a pin in her mouth, but she still managed to speak. Elisabeth smirked as she looks at her. Neither of them is a gossip and it is slightly out of character for either of them to ask such a question.
"Just Navarre chasing tennis balls and Guise tossing his hair." Marie pulled her lips into a grimace at my bluntness.
"Is Catherine all right? Is she sitting comfortably?" Out of the three of us, Marie does not have any children yet, but she is determined to make up for that lack by accompanying our sister to her laying-in. She's started to hover around her in anticipation of playing nursemaid.
"She's fine," I took a seat and tried to pick up a corner to start stitching. Marie's stitches are impressive. She's making up for lost time as she grew up a Protestant in Navarre with our aunt, the Queen of Navarre. Since converting to Catholicism, Marie is determined to stitch every altar cloth in France.
"I don't miss the last months of pregnancy. I waddled everywhere and I had to constantly sit down in order to catch my breath." The Queen is known for her kindness and compassion, which is why she has no enemies in court. It is also why she has few friends because she has failed to supply the court with its lifeblood, scandal and gossip.
"Marie, are you sure that you want to go to Joinville? It's a long trip?" I'm being selfish, I know. I don't want to lose two of my sisters and be left alone in Paris. The court will leave next week to follow the Duc d'Anjou, the newly elected King of Poland and the

King's younger brother to the French border to wish the new monarch well. Anjou is completely besotted with my sister and she spends as many hours as possible in his company.

"I promised Catherine I would help her out and I won't go back on my promise. Besides," she blushed a deep red, "I want to say goodbye to Anjou." After saying that, she suddenly became very interested in her embroidery and fell silent.

"My husband is happy to get the King of Poland to his subjects. I think that France is a little too small with two kings." Elisabeth deftly summed up the sibling rivalry between King Charles and his younger brother. Anjou tarried despite the King's efforts to almost move heaven and earth to get him to the Poles. The news of Anjou's election to the Polish throne came while the royal army worked to subdue the city of La Rochelle and its rebellion against royal authority. The king faced a choice of continuing to fund the siege of La Rochelle or pay to have his brother conveniently out of the country for the foreseeable future. The price the King paid in ending a successful siege against Protestant rebels was too high and he regretted paying it almost immediately.

"Besides, Conde can't complain that I'm being immoral if I'm in a room with a woman giving birth." Marie rolled her eyes and started stabbing the cloth with her needle.

"He's claiming that you're unfaithful? When the entire court knows the opposite to be true?"

"Yes, I can hear him drone on and on all the way from Picardy. Apparently, Paris is a bad influence on me and he thinks going to the countryside and away from bad influences will do me well."

I was the "bad influence" that had Conde so riled up. The rivalry between Anjou and the Prince of Conde stemmed from years of ill-gotten military appointments. The Queen Mother snatched command of the French armies from Conde's father, who in truth was more qualified to lead troops than Anjou would ever prove to be. Conde was convinced that Anjou flirted with Marie only to get under his skin. Louis and I had insisted that Marie stay under our roof while Conde left to govern Picardy so that her reputation would remain unsullied. Nothing could deter Anjou from writing amorous letters to my sister, however. Conde was convinced that since I did nothing to stop those letters from coming into my home, then I must be encouraging my sister to cuckold him. Conde's paranoia was exhausting, but Marie was determined to follow her heart and remain loyal to her husband. How she juggled the two men was beyond me.

"How is your son, Madame de Nevers?" a polite and innocent question, asked by one without malice. Elisabeth of Austria simply meant to be polite, but her kindness caused me to tear up. I would prefer the cruelty and cutting remarks of the court to the bit of kindness that the Queen offered.

I shook my head, "No better. We've called in every surgeon we could think of, but no one seems to be able to help him." The tears overtook me and I shook with sobs. Marie jumped to her feet and held me in her arms.

"Forgive me, Madame. I should not have upset you." Like her compassion, Elisabeth's remorse was genuine. "I can offer nothing other than my prayers, and you and your family are in them."

God had not deigned to answer my prayers, but maybe he would listen to Elisabeth's. I simply nodded and tried to mouth a "thank you" while Marie held me.

"Tonight will be much smaller than last time. I can't deal with another boring recitation from another subpar actor." Claude Catherine pulled me through the rooms of her vast hotel, a building so massive that it managed to dwarf even mine. I needed this distraction, after several sleepless nights at Frederick's bedside, able to do nothing more than hold his hand. I had thought that by holding vigil at his bedside, I might prove to God that I deserved to have my son healed. Perhaps God would see that I was worthy of His compassion and He would take pity on us both and heal him. To my disappointment, my bargaining with God did no good; Frederick was no better.

I decided to plunge into the distractions provided by our usual salons to cheer myself up. Avoiding my pain did nothing, nor did facing it head on. My face must have darkened at the thought because Claude looked at me, "Are you sure that you're up to this?"

I gave her a quick nod, "It's better than crying myself to sleep." I felt isolated and unable to confess my dark feelings to any of my friends. I could hardly tell Margot what I was feeling, as she had yet to have her first child. Try as she might, the princess could not understand the terror I felt in the idea of losing my son. Claude knew little of what I was going through as her children were healthy and robust. Margot had yet to give birth to her first child. I could hardly count on either of them to fully understand what I was going through. Sympathy and compassion were one thing, experiencing the same thing was another.

Claude clapped her hands, "Good! I'll seat you next to some disgustingly handsome man who can carry on a conversation." She winked at me and bounded off to direct the servants in last minute preparations.

As it turned out, Claude Catherine seated me next to Annibal de Coconnas, who was more than willing to continue our conversation from the other evening. "Madame, I'm told that you're something of a financial genius," he turned to me. He chose the right form of seduction, if that was what he was doing. I would not be seduced with flowery words about my beauty or grace, but an appeal to my intellect got my attention.

"When I became the Duchess, most of our land was tied up in the Empire and extricating their revenue wasn't the easiest of tasks." This wasn't false humility; we Cleves were faithful subjects of the Holy Roman Emperor and had Phillip of Spain fulfilled his father's promises to us, we would have remained subjects of the Empire. My father unfortunately learned how duplicitous Spain could be just before his death and there was little that he could do to get the money due us from our loyalty to the Spanish crown. We were forced to throw in our lot with Francis I, becoming French subjects. My father's marriage to a Bourbon cemented our alliance to the France.

"It's a rare person who can make or keep a fortune these days." He leaned in towards me.

"Are you under the impression that flattery will get you anywhere?" Was he teasing me? If he thought he was dealing with an empty-headed demoiselle, he was mistaken.

He shook his head, "No, it's not empty flattery. I'm impressed with what you've done."

"Then, I suppose I should return your compliment? Mine don't come so easily." I smiled at him, determined that he would understand my warning that I would not be an easy conquest.

He fingered the flute of the glass before him. I could not stop from admiring those fingers, at how deftly he circled the hard planes of the pattern. I started to wonder how they would feel against my skin. The months of strained encounters meant that Louis and I had not spent an evening together for longer than I could count. I missed the sensation of physical contact more than I realized.

Coconnas noticed me staring at his hands, curse the man! I was trapped and I could not talk my way out of this situation. Years of watching Margot take advantage of sexually charged moments suddenly came to my rescue. "I wonder, Monsieur, why you are not with the rest of the court on your way to Lorraine. Is there a special reason why you are compelled to stay here in Paris?" The double entendre was blatant. I had already gone too far already, staring at him openly. I could not stop now and there was no saving myself or claiming innocence.

He smiled, unwilling to let the fact that I was staring go unnoticed. "Most of the Duc d'Alceon's retinue followed him with the King of Poland and the Queen Mother. I, however, must stay in Paris to take care of the Duc's business. My associate, Boniface La Mole," he glanced at Margot, who looked virtually naked without a male admirer at her side, "keeps me updated daily on the activities in Lorraine."

His knowing glance at Margot told me that she and La Mole were more of an item than I had initially suspected. Margot had not confessed to me who her most recent lover was, but since my mind was occupied with my son's condition, Margot seemed almost embarrassed to regale me with the details of a frivolous love affair.

"Madame de Nevers, it is becoming insufferably hot in this dining room. There are no more courses to be eaten. I suggest that we take in some cooler air." Perhaps the heat had gotten to me, because a cooler head would've stayed rooted in the room, far away from this man's advances. Too caught up in my sudden attraction, I could not say no to him. I simply nodded and followed him out into the hallway of the hotel

Once we were outside, the crisp November air bit at my arms and I pulled my cape around me. In a graceful and sweeping motion, Coconnas removed his own cape and offered it to me. Once again, common sense deserted me and I accepted it with a shy smile. Bereft of his own cloak, he began to walk directly beside me as we strolled around the courtyard of Claude's home.

"I understand that your husband is a close advisor to the new King of Poland."

"Are you really going to talk politics to me now?" I grinned, once again unable to resist teasing him.

He gave a low chuckle, "No, I'm simply trying to determine how dangerous a seduction will be for me; and for my patron. His Highness enjoys the support of the Protestant and the Malcontents in the court." The Malcontents, a derogatory term given to the Catholics who opposed the idea of the Duc d'Anjou taking the throne upon the current King's death. Both parties would gladly push Anjou from the French succession the moment he left France for his Polish throne.

"As Louis's wife, you think that I am also Anjou's creature?" I shrugged, "The Duc is currently in love with my sister, so it would be to my advantage to support him as well."

"You're being very philosophical, so I assume that you aren't as enamored with Anjou."

I let out a small breath. "I believe that France will get the King that she gets; jostling for position before it's necessary is useless."

He guffawed, "A very political answer, Madame!"

I grinned, "How do you think I was able to become as rich as I am now?'

Before he could answer, a burst of riotous laughter drifted out of an open window. I looked up, distracted by the sound. Coconnas took advantage of the moment to grab my forearm and pull me into an alcove. There, hidden in the shadows, he kissed me passionately. I did not mind his actions one bit.

"Until the next time, Madame Nevers." He tipped his hat to me and led me out of the shadows and back to the dining room.

Frederick continued to linger on, getting no better. The expert physician from Turin advised us that a change of environment was the only thing that could save him. "The clear air of the countryside can only heal him. Much of Paris is a squalor," he cleared his throat when he saw the murderous look in my eye and hastened to add. "Of course, the Duc's home is a bastion of luxury, but the air here in Paris is not healthy for a child with a diseased body."

I had no desire to send my only son away where I could not take care of him myself, but Louis was insistent. "If it is the best for him, then we must do it, Henriette." As always, he appealed to my logical side, instead of my emotions. Louis was uncomfortable with the emotional side of an argument, which could make it difficult to argue with him sometimes. It also made it difficult for him to understand the agony I felt at the idea of being separated from Frederick. I had carried the boy inside my body and he still felt as if he were a part of me. As a man, Louis could not understand the bond between mother and son and the pain of physical separation.

We settled on sending him to our home in Nevers, our Ducal seat where he would be treated with every luxury imaginable. "I'll even go with him, so that I can ensure that he is settled in comfortably."

"I'll go with you, then," I started, but Louis cut me off mid-sentence.

"No, I can take care of our son. One of us must see to our affairs in Paris."

That irked me, Louis thought that of the two of us he was more suited to seeing our son to his sickbed. "Then, I should go with him while you remain here at court."

18

"Henriette, you're too emotional now and I'm afraid that you'd upset the boy."

"If he's sick, then he needs his mother around him."

"I'll have more authority if I see to the move to Nevers."

That further infuriated me, Nevers was my own duchy, which I inherited from my father. Louis was Duke only by his marriage to me. Did he really think that now was the time to usurp my authority?

"Louis, you are being unreasonable and furthermore, you are insulting me." My face grew redder with each word. Like my sisters, my pale complexion meant that it was impossible to hide my anger.

He blew air out of his pursed lips. "Anjou has asked me to ensure that you remain close to Margot. He and the Queen Mother are convinced that she and Alceon are plotting to push Alceon to the throne during his absence in Poland."

"And you expect me to spy for them? You really think that is more important than caring for my son?" The idea was absurd. I was shouting, but Louis' lack of emotions made me more determined to display my own.

He sat down wordlessly. Finally, he spoke in soft tones, as if he were trying to calm a spooked horse. "Henriette, I have no desire to upset you, but you must see the bigger picture. You lost both of your brothers and there's a chance that we could lose our son as well. If he is gone, we will have to court the next King's favor so that one of our daughters can inherit."

He was right, of course. The logic of his strategy caused tears to prick at my eyes. "I can't think of the idea of losing Frederick." I looked at my husband, my face a blotched and swollen mess. He looked just as defeated as I felt.

"I will hover over him the entire time that I am there." I could only nod and walk out of the room. Emotions kept me from embracing him and I could feel the gulf between us widening. No matter how dire the situation, we still could not manage to unite in our time of grief.

Thus, by the time that the Advent season began in 1573, I was alone in Paris, bereft of my sisters, my son and my husband. The loneliness was unbearable.

Loneliness and isolation could only be alleviated by a pleasurable diversion and Margot was more than willing to aid me in finding one. "Louis is away and I think that you should take advantage of the situation to begin an affair." Her eyes sparkled with the prospect of an illicit relationship, one that was very close to her. "Mole will be back in Paris in a few days and I can help you find time with Coconnas." She slapped her forehead, "What am I saying—you have that cavernous house all to yourself, so *of course* you can find time to be with him."

"Marie will be back soon and I can't kick my own sister out of my home." Margot was cleverer than that, how could she forget that my sister lived virtually homeless with her homely husband away in Picardy? She must have some plan afoot.

"You practically helped Marie and Anjou begin their relationship, so she owes you the favor." Margot was overstating my role in Marie and Anjou's odd flirtation: all I had done was reroute letters between the two and look the other way when they met in person at our home. Margot and Anjou were constantly at one another's throat, so the scandal her brother raised by openly flirting with my sister gave Margot a perverse pleasure. Outwardly, the Queen Mother expected an unapprochably moral court; the reality was that we all took our pleasure where we could find it.

I had resisted temptation for years, but my attraction to Coconnas was irresistible. Fed up with the strained civility between Louis and I, the passion I felt for Coconnas was the balm I needed while I stretched thin with apprehension over my son. Meeting my lover at the Hotel de Nevers would certainly violate the Queen Mother's double standard of propriety, so Margot and I devised a plan to meet him in the chambers assigned to Alceon's retainers.

Within weeks, we contrived to spend as much time in one another's company as possible. My time with him was the highlight of each day. I once again felt desired and carefree, feelings that lay dormant for too many months. Although I came into this affair determined to be discreet, soon I grew less cautious in our meetings. I'm sure that it was not long before word spread throughout the hallways of the Louvre that we were lovers.

Lying in his arms one chilly December afternoon, we watched the fire lick at the embers in front of us. "Alceon and Navarre are planning to escape from the court," he whispered to me. I rolled over onto my stomach and propped my chin on his chest.

"Are they both mad? The King may spend most of his time in bed, but his guards never take their eyes off either of them."

He tilted his head back, acknowledging my point. "The King vomits up blood with his consumption, meaning that his time is near. Once Anjou hears that he is King, he will race back to France. Alceon plans to be ready to face his older brother with his own army."

Placing my palms on each of his hips, I pushed myself up. "What army?"

"There are troops in Champagne, outside of Reims." Reims, the ancient coronation place of the French kings. Champagne, territory controlled by the Guise family. If Alceon could position his troops in time, he could surround his older brother and force him to forfeit the crown. If the coup succeeded, my liaison with Coconnas would be beneficial, but if it failed, thank God Louis was Anjou's closest advisor outside of the Royal Family.

A second later, I realized that if I knew about the conspiracy, then it was likely that many others in the court did, too. "Does Margot know about this plot?" She had not mentioned it to me, but continued to hide things from me; a misguided attempt to avoid adding to my burdens.

He shook his head, "She's been kept in the dark. Alceon knows that she can't show him favor and that she's torn between her brothers. He needs her as an ally, whether he takes the throne from Anjou or if he later finds himself at Anjou and the Queen Mother's mercy."

He said no more and unwilling to spoil the rest of the day with talk of politics, we turned to more carnal matters. I had thought that the exertion would distract me and calm my mind, but when I returned home that evening, I began to feel unsettled. I had to speak to

Margot and as soon as possible.

First thing the next morning, I marched into Margot's audience chamber, a small space given to her as a ceremonial favor as Queen of Navarre. I had hoped to find her alone, but as I entered, I heard a deep male voice speaking. The man was insistent, his voice high and strained. I could not make out the words, so feigning ignorance, I continued to walk into the chamber.

Margot was deep in conversation with her husband's own chancellor, Monsieur de Miossans.

The rest of her retinue were nowhere in sight and a lesser woman would have turned her heel and left her presence to give them privacy. I knew that no matter what the two were conversing about, Margot would prefer that I remain. Miossans and Margot shared a history as he was one of the Protestant men who staggered into Margot's bedchamber and begged her for sanctuary during the bloodbath that occurred on St. Bartholomew's Day. He knew Margot was made of steel and that he could trust her with his own life. We were likely the only two people in France who were assured of such special access to the Queen of Navarre.

"The forces are determined to regroup at Champagne." I could only see the back of his head, but Margot's face was grave. She gave him her full attention and simply nodded. He continued to give her the full story of the conspiracy, all of it the same as what Coconnas had told me the afternoon before.

"You're sure that my brother is determined to go through with this?" Margot was no fool; she knew who to trust and who to dismiss with a wave of her white hands.

"I've heard the same thing, Margot. I came here to tell you the same thing, but I see that I've been superseded." At the sound of my voice, Miossans turned and looked at me, his mouth agape.

"They're been exceedingly careless in the plot and far too many people know about it already. It's best that we do something to save them from themselves."

Margot knew full well how I had heard of the plot, but she kept that detail to herself. Tapping her fingers on the arm of her chair, she began to weigh her options. "Even if they succeed, and it's doubtful that they will, my brother and Navarre will be in open rebellion against the King and Anjou. I've sacrificed too much to allow them to do something so stupid. Keep your ears open and if you hear anything else, let me know. I'll figure out what needs to be done."

He bowed to her, grateful that once again she did not violate his trust in her. Like me, he knew that Margot was a valuable ally. Once he was gone, she turned to me.

"I'll have to prostrate myself in order to get them both out of trouble. I suppose now my husband will expect me to save him from the hangman's noose every time he makes a stupid decision." She rolled her eyes in disgust and rising, began to pace the room. I knew from her actions that she was formulating a plan.

"I have little to bargain with, but can offer the King this promise: if he will promise to spare Navarre and our brother, I will tell him of the plot. It may be the only way that I can save both of them from death."

"What do you need me to do?"

"I need you to go with me to my mother's audience chamber." She signaled for a page, "Send word to the Queen Mother that I must speak to her immediately. It is a matter of life and death."

I stood outside Catherine de Medici's presence chamber as Margot detailed the plot to her brother and her mother. In the end, her plan worked, Navarre and Alceon escaped death by Margot's persuasion.

Word arrived from Nevers, bearing my husband's seal. Our son was improving slightly, which meant that the physician's advice to send him there was sound. Louis wrote that he regretted that say that the physician advised that our son set up his household at Nevers, while Louis would need to return to Paris and to the King's service as soon as possible. I realized that I was prudent in keeping my meetings with Coconnas outside of our home. Once my husband returned, I would not have to go through the intricacies of finding alternative meeting places. The times spent with my lover were too precious to me, and I had no desire to give them up.

By the end of December, a letter arrived from my sister Marie. Catherine had given birth to a stillborn girl and my heart broke for my sister over the loss of her tiny daughter. I hoped that the infant's death was not a portent of Frederick's own demise and prayed that death had touched our family enough. Marie's letter went on to say that instead of returning to Paris, she would leave immediately for Picardy to visit her insufferable husband. I dared hope that my sister had finally grown a backbone and she went to demand a divorce from the Prince de Conde in person. Once rid of her husband, there might be hope of Marie marrying Anjou, or failing that, to become his mistress. A royal mistress enjoyed power unmatched by all but a Queen Mother of a child King.

Margot had wrenched an additional promise from the King that he would not give Navarre or Alceon any indication how he had learned of the plot. The Queen Mother had another tactic when dealing with both men; she assigned Madame de Sauve to expand her duties in the bedchamber to include a seduction of Alceon. The ungainly and pockmarked eighteen-year-old prince was far too enthralled with the guiles of de Sauve's seduction to bother to wonder why she suddenly turned her attentions towards him. For Navarre's part, I don't know if my cousin bothered to think about his mistress' newfound attentions towards his unattractive brother-in-law.

In fact, each man seemed to look upon keeping Charlotte de Sauve's affections as kind of a game, jostling for her attention and keeping score as if they were on a tennis court. The scandal and merriment that the two gave the court took attention away from Margot and myself, and we took the opportunity to continue our own affairs without much interference. Apparently, as far as gossip went, we were much less interesting for the wagging tongues of the court.

My ever-practical husband no doubt learned that I had a lover as soon as he returned to Paris, if not sooner, but if he felt anger or jealousy, he said nothing. My sisters might have husbands prone to fits of jealous rage, but Louis simply accepted my betrayal of our marriage vows as a matter of course. He was too busy playing a diplomatic game of simultaneously serving the dying King and his likely successor, the Duc d'Anjou. Letters arrived daily from Poland, most of them addressed to Louis and the rest addressed to Marie. Using our surreptitious method, I re-routed them to Picardy while I waited for her return to Paris.

Guilt-ridden and looking for allies, the Duc d'Alceon stayed close to Margot, which meant that we were able to see an increasing amount of Mole and Coconnas. In fact, the remaining Valois gathered closely together at the Chateau St. Germain, a day's ride out of the squalor of Paris. The King's own physician advised him to stay at the chateau until his health improved. The Queen Mother took a particular interest in improving the gardens of the chateau, making it one of the most Italian of the royal palaces. I took advantage of the new surroundings and took every opportunity to spend time with Coconnas.

The court's move to St. Germain meant that my sister Catherine made her return to court after healing from the loss of her daughter. I was determined to repair our relationship, due in part to my selfish fear that death would take my own child. Death took those under the age of five years all too often in those days and I hung on with superstitious hope that I could ward off the same fate for Frederick. Although my days and nights were filled with enough activity and concern, if I could manage to make amends with my sister, I hoped I would feel some relief from my guilt.

The lingering resentment over our inheritance meant that our conversations were awkward and that chilly January, Catherine and I stuck to familiar topics, or at least those familiar to each of us. "I have to admit, I was shocked to hear that you had taken on a lover," she remarked one day as we looked out over the gardens of the palace from her apartment windows. Most days, she walked around in a lingering melancholy, but on that day, the color began to return to her cheeks.

"Were you under the impression that I was incapable of doing so?" I tried to make my voice sound teasing and not harsh, but I could still hear the defensiveness in my tone.

She shook her head, chastened momentarily, "No, it's just that in all the years that you've been married, I never heard of you having the least interest in another man. And I," she gave me a wicked smile, "hear everything that goes on in the court."

"I'm sure you do!" I laughed, grateful that we had broken the iciness between us.

"So, what is it, boredom?" Her question was without malice, more of a sisterly concern. Still, it bothered me, unused as I was to the idea of confessing my romantic feelings for another man. Perhaps I still felt some guilt over my actions.

"I feel plagued by anguish and fear these days. I wanted to feel relief for a while. That's what Coconnas does for me." I need not explain any more to Catherine, who daily mourned the loss of a child. Only another mother could understand the apprehension that I felt on a daily basis, the nervousness and the constant bargaining with God to keep my child safe. Catherine knew firsthand what it felt like when God refused to make a bargain.

"Can you really not talk to Louis?" The question hung in the air and I could not answer it. I had asked myself the same question several times before and always came up with a different answer. Catherine pressed on, unnerved by the silence.

"He is a cold fish, I'll give you that. Perhaps he doesn't know how to speak to you." She lifted her eyebrows and inclined her head in my direction. That was my sister, always convinced that there was an easy answer to a problem, if one looked hard enough to find it.

"Catherine, Louis isn't as excitable as your husband. I've seen the two of you going at it, having a row. And he isn't the kind to let things fester. In fact, I wouldn't be surprised if Guise lost his temper one day and you or your lover wound up dead."

She shrugged, unwilling to concede my point. "At least we would have a solution. What good is sitting around in silence?"

Too stubborn to answer her, I stared silently ahead of me. "Perhaps you are ignoring Louis as a way of punishing him?"

"Why would I possibly punish him? Frederick is his son, too."

"Wasn't it his idea to send him to Nevers?" Curse my sister, was there nothing that went on in my private household that she was not aware of? Catherine was becoming a bigger gossip with age. "Having an affair right under his nose would be a particularly effective way of getting him back for separating you from your son."

"You make him sound like a tyrant; and you're making *me* sound like one, too." I was growing tired of her prying questions.

"You are much closer to Nevers here at St. Germain. No one would fault you for riding out to check on Frederick for a few days."

No matter how much Catherine irked me, I had to admit that she might be at least partially right. When I entered our shared apartments, Louis was in the sitting room, looking over papers. "I'm going to Nevers for a few days to check on Frederick. If there's any change in his progress, I'll write you immediately."

Louis looked up from his work, dazed. "That sounds good." I waited for him to add anything more, a jealous quip under his breath. An accusation that I was leaving to rendezvous with my lover. Anything that might indicate that he might feel jealousy over the loss of our intimacy. He said nothing and my heart sank.

When I got to my sister Marie's apartments, she was also working on her correspondence and when she saw me, she gave a jump and shoved the papers away like a guilty child. "Ah, I see the post for Poland is coming soon."

"Ah, yes. I wanted to finish this before supper." One of the papers slipped out of the snarled pile she had hastily made and glided onto the floor. Marie pretended not to notice it.

"Really, Marie?"

She cleared her throat and gave me a false smile. I had no desire to know what kind of overly wrought words of devotion she was sending to Anjou, yet her discomfort was fun to watch. If I were not in the midst of packing to see my son, I would stay and see if she would squirm guiltily in her chair for much longer.

"I'm leaving first thing tomorrow for Nevers to see to Frederick."

Her face drained of color, "Is he all right?"

I put my hand up to calm her, noticing that since returning from

Picardy, her moods were becoming erratic. I made a note to speak to her after I returned to Paris.

"He's fine, I simply miss him." At that, she smiled and I returned her goodwill gesture.

"The Queen Mother asked that I stay close to Queen Elisabeth while the King is ailing, so I don't know when I will be back to Hotel de Nevers."

Louis would be in our massive home by himself, left to his own devices. If he chose, he could take on a mistress and I would be none the wiser for it. I felt a quick pang of jealousy at the thought. The feeling reminded me that I would need to speak to Coconnas before I left. I hated to tell him goodbye, but I would not leave without a proper farewell.

"I need to pack. Keep an eye on Catherine for me, will you? I think she'll be up to her usual mischievousness before too long." I could not help but smile at the idea.

"I hope so."

I stayed in Nevers until the end of February, enjoying the quiet and spending as much time with my son as I could. Every mother hopes for a chubby happy baby, but I only wished for a healthy one. Much of my guilt faded away as I saw that Frederick indeed had the best care possible at Nevers as the Florentine specialist spent his waking hours hovering over him and doing all he could do to bring my son to health.

Eventually, part of my anger at Louis for his decision to send the boy away began to fade. I was able to forgive him for what at the time had felt like a heartless decision. I certainly spent enough hours in Mass and at prayer doing my own bargaining for my child's life. In moments of great self-sacrifice, I offered to give up Coconnas in order to save my child and in others, I selfishly reverted to my desire to remain in Coconnas' arms. Torn between selfishness and guilt, I could not make the decision to keep Coconnas or let him go. Eventually, I decided that whether I ended our relationship or not, it would likely make little difference to God.

By March, I returned home to Paris and the Hotel de Nevers. Our home was a picture of domestic tranquility. Louis and Marie had managed the household quite handily without me. "I'm quite impressed, Marie. If you ever manage to get a home of your own, you'll be quite the chatelaine."

To my horror, my sister burst into tears. I had only been home for hours and already had an emotional woman on my hands. "Dearest, whatever is the matter?" I led her to a chair in the parlor, where she sank down with a long sigh. For the next several moments, she sobbed uncontrollably while I watched her helplessly.

"I just found out the other day, I'm pregnant."

The full horror of what she was telling me hit before I could pull my face into a bland expression. "Please tell me it's Anjou's child."

She looked at me with a mix of rage and annoyance. For the first time, I realized how much my sisters favored one another. She was the very image of Catherine when she got into one of her emotional states. "No, it's my husband's!"

It's quite possible that my sister was the only woman in France who would be devastated at the idea of having her husband's legitimate child and heir. To be honest, we were all horrified at the idea of her having Conde's child. A pregnancy would prove once and for all to the Vatican that their ill-considered marriage was consummated. If Marie hoped to divorce Conde and later marry Anjou, this could be the end of her hopes.

"How could you? I thought you went to Picardy to ask for a divorce."

"No, I went to, I mean—I had to talk to him and I thought..." she looked flustered and I remembered the day before I left for Nevers and I realized that she was obviously hiding something from me. "I felt guilty about Anjou and I decided to try to fix our marriage." she squeaked out.

There was little I could say to her to make her feel better. "Well, another Prince de Conde is good for the succession, I suppose." It was a weak attempt, but it was all that either of us could think of that was good in her current situation. She was trapped for now until the child came or she lost it.

"I hope you're doing better with your situation," she attempted a thin smile and I hugged her. "As a matter of fact, I am meeting Coconnas tomorrow at Margot's apartments. Alceon has arranged a little get together in honor of my return."

Officially, the reason for the day's fete was to welcome me back to Paris, in fact, the Duc d'Alceon was determined to ingratiate himself with his sister as much as possible. Someone, most likely Coconnas, had apparently told Alceon that Margot informed the King during their latest plot to escape and Alceon realized that he needed Margot's support now more than ever. Finally, the Queen of Navarre was considered to be a power player within the French court and she relished her newly elevated status.

"I'm being courted by my brother and ignored by my husband. I really can't complain about my situation." Margot strutted around her apartments, relishing the attention. My relationship with Coconnas picked up where we left it, but he stopped talking to me about politics. That was just as well with me since our hours together were the only hours of respite I got from my increasing family issues. I wanted passionate, light-hearted entertainment from my lover and he was willing to provide it. If Alceon expected his man to garner any information about Margot's plans from me, Coconnas declined to do so as we laid naked in one another's arms.

I suppose that was why I was taken by complete surprise one day in April when word spread throughout Saint Germain that a Protestant army was spotted heading directly towards the chateau. Unlike most royal residences, Saint Germain was built more like a country villa, reminiscent of those the Medici built in Italy. Situated on a hill, the chateau had few natural defenses. The menace of an invading army was something that the Valois would not take lightly.

When I heard the panicked shouts, I was bereft of all of my clothing and snuggled closely to Coconnas. Once he heard the word "attack," he jumped from the bed and to his feet. "Those fools! They're too early!"

"What are you talking about? My blonde curls askew as always, I tried to smooth them back into a quick braid. Fishing around for my clothing, I dressed as quickly as possible and rang for my lady's maid. While I waited for her arrival, my lover abruptly exited the bedchamber. With no regard to my appearance, I began to search the frenzied halls of the chateau in search of my husband. I found him mustering troops. "What on earth is going on?"

"It's the Politiques and the Protestants," he spat. "They've decided not to have the decency to wait for the King to meet his Heavenly reward and simply take the crown now. And since they couldn't break Navarre and Alceon out of the chateau, they'll simply bring an army to them."

An entire army marching towards us! I could not image the carnage. "What is the King to do?"

"He's in no shape to do much of anything. The Queen Mother has ordered out the Swiss Guard." It was so like Catherine de Medici to deal with a crisis by sending out the most fearsome soldiers in all of France. Marie was likely with the Queen Mother, so I would not have to worry about her safety. That left my sister Catherine. "I'll go find Catherine."

"Guise wants her to evacuate as soon as possible and heading to safety at Joinville. If you hurry, you can catch her."

"Louis, where should I go?"

He gave me a quick nod, "Go to Nevers and see to our son." It was the best idea that I had heard in months and it took no convincing for me to agree. The weeks we'd spent apart were far too long. But first, I had to check on my sister.

I ran at top speed to my sister's apartments, finding her directing her servants to pack anything of value. "My husband's uncles," she said, referring to the Cardinals of Lorraine and Guise, "are halfway to Nancy by now. The moment they heard we were under attack, they jumped on their horses and ran away like a couple of dowager aunts." Despite her panic, she found the idea of the men gathering up their skirts and running for their lives quite comical.

"Marie is barricaded behind the walls of the Queen Mother's apartments. No one is allowed in or out other than royal messengers. She's safe, though," she added.

31

"I'll check on Margot and then I'll start packing for Nevers." The chance to see my son again buoyed me and despite the dire situation, I did feel buoyed by the prospect. Now was not the time to celebrate, however, and I tempered my reaction.

Hastening to Margot's chambers, I noticed that there was no rush to pack. Margot stood in the middle of her audience chamber, much calmer than I would have expected. "Are you planning on staying?" It was not a ridiculous question; Margot had survived much worse than this.

"My Mother has the invaders engaged and she's ordered the entire court to go to Vincennes." She rolled her eyes, as if the entire situation were nothing more than an inconvenience.

The chateau of Vincennes was the closest and most heavily fortified royal residence within riding distance of Saint Germain. If the court could make it there in time, we could hold out against all but the mightiest army. My heart sank as I realized that I would not be going to visit my son after all. No one would be allowed on the roads for fear of spies or the danger of becoming valuable hostages for the Protestants.

"I don't suppose anyone has bothered to tell the Cardinals of Lorraine and Guise about this plan?" I remarked drily. I was beginning to see Margot's point; this evacuation would quickly become one great inconvenience.

"Those old women! I'm sure they're halfway to Lorraine by now. And good riddance!" She doubled over in laughter at the idea of the two elderly men making all haste to escape an army while the rest of the court went in the opposite direction.

"Margot, you're terrible!" My attempt to chastise her ended in a burst of laughter. She smiled at me like a naughty school girl.

The movement of a royal court, even one that is planned out in advance, is a chaotic and stressful event. A court running for its life is a nightmare and for the seventeen miles between St. Germain and Vincennes, we sprinted for the safety of the fortress on the outskirts of Paris. No one had time to make preparations for us and once we got to Vincennes, the compound was in chaos as well.

With no real apartments or living spaces for the courtiers, we were packed into shared rooms, more irritable than fearful. The entire situation was miserable and I was particularly annoyed that I had been denied the opportunity to spend the time with my son at Nevers. At least our daughters were safe with their governess back at the Hotel de Nevers.

Catherine and the Duc de Guise shared chambers with us, which was less awkward since we had buried our quarrel months earlier. "I hear that Charlotte de Sauve is having more trouble than usual keeping both Navarre and Alceon at bay this time. They're both terrified that the King will send them to the gallows any moment." Faced with nothing more to do for the next two weeks, as spring rains came in late March, we kept amused eyes on Madame de Sauve and her attempts to juggle her two anxious lovers.

In order to save his own neck and stave off exile, the Duc d'Alceon fell to his knees a day after we arrived in Vincennes to confess the entire plot to his mother. The prince and Navarre knew that the odds of being forgiven were against them and we all waited on tenterhooks to see how the King and his mother would deal with their rebellion. Even as jaded and cynical as we all were, none of us guessed the lengths that the two princes would go to in order to save their own lives.

Jammed up against one another, finding places to secretly meet with one's paramour became difficult to manage. The King and Guise decided to make great sport of the situation one day by lying in wait to see if he could catch my lover coming out of my apartments. I may have been reckless during those days, but I was not stupid. Early one cold spring morning, I opened the door on my way to Margot's chambers to find the King and my brother-in-law grinning like idiots.

"May I help you, Sire? Brother?"

"Where is he?" Guise managed to speak, while the King giggled like a young girl.

"If you're looking for Louis, he is not here." I crossed my arms and started at both of them.

"Madame, we are looking for Monsieur la Mole," the King

managed through giggles.

"He is not here, as you can see. Perhaps," a door clicked at the end of the hallway. We all turned to see the gentleman in question tiptoeing out of Margot's chambers.

"If you'll excuse me, I have to attend the Queen." I pushed past both of them, ignoring their laughter. Even when proven wrong, the two could find nothing other than humor in the situation.

Sighing, I strode into Margot's chambers. "Margot, the King and Guise are at spying on women's bedchambers. They saw Mole creeping out of your chambers." While I was angry and annoyed at the intrusion upon my privacy, Margot simply shrugged her shoulders.

"Guise and my brother should be careful if they plan on rifling through someone's private belongings. They never know what they might find."

By April, we settled in the Chateau de Fountainbleu, the Queen Mother refusing to give into the threat of an army and the King annoyed at the idea of a return to Paris proper. Still, the tasteless games and spying continued, carried on by the Queen Mother's Flying Squadron of female agents. My nerves frayed, I took out my annoyance on Charlotte de Sauve one afternoon as we attended upon the Queen Mother. "I have heard, Madame, that you are spending much of your time sneaking about the apartments of the men of the court. Are your lovers not enough to satisfy you?"

She stiffened and her face became hard as stone. "My activities are none of your business, Madame de Nevers. I serve Her Majesty the Queen Mother and answer only to her." Her prim voice instantly grated on my nerves.

"Then, I suppose we should hide all of our valuables, then? I wonder, just what would you do with them?" The accusation hit her hard, her family was newly raised and had no noble blood whatsoever. Her father's title of Viscount and her husband's new title of Baron de Sauve came through service to the Crown, a reflection of their need to keep a constant influx of money in order to stay at court. Worse still, without the intricate intermarriages of families that established nobles boasted, she had no network of cousins or uncles to speak for her when she was in danger of falling from favor with the Valois.

"My family has not fallen upon hard times as many of the so-called 'noble' houses have." She nodded towards the impoverished Countess de Limourges, who lived only on the charity of her sister, a Duchesse.

"Nobility carries with it a certain adherence to propriety. I doubt you could manage to purchase that." At that, I stood up and moved to the window. I was so arrogant that day, thinking that I had scored a victory over her. Little did I know, I had secured a death warrant for the man who made my moments sweeter.

Days after my encounter with Madame de Sauve, we heard a ruckus from the direction of the rooms where La Mole, Coconnas and other gentlemen of Alceon's retinue were housed in the Tuileries. While the palace afforded more room than Vincennes, few of us were afforded much privacy. Outside of my antechamber, I heard the Swiss Guard rushing down the hallway. Thinking that we were moments away from another escape to Vincennes, I asked a passing maid what was the cause of the commotion.

"My Lady, the guards say that there is another conspiracy at the court. The Protestants and Catholics have joined to kill the king." Unable to leave or attack, apparently, the conspirators had decided to simply rid themselves of the king. I had no desire to follow the growing crowd that followed the Swiss Guard, but at my elbow, my husband's page spoke up. "Madame, they are going towards Monsieur La Mole's quarters."

Knowing that Margot would likely be in the crowd in order to position herself to defend her lover, I decided that I should join the throng after all. Reaching for my shawl, I blended into the rush of silks as it passed down the hall.

"I tell you, I am innocent!" Mole's voice echoed from his chambers. Before I could open my mouth, I heard Margot's voice.

"Whatever is going on?" she demanded with all of the haughtiness that came with being born the daughter of a king.

The excited crowd buzzed the word from La Mole's doorway to Margot's position in the middle of the hall, "It is a wax figure of the King!"

One overly excited woman shrieked, "Le Mole means to kill the King!"

"Mon Dieu!" Half of the assembled crowd hastily crossed themselves. As I glanced at those who did not do so, I noticed Charlotte de Sauve, looking suspiciously calm.

The guard dragged La Mole out into the hallway and we could only watch as they took him away. Margot crooked her finger at me and I quickly followed her to her chambers. We stayed there until late that night, when one of her pages finally gave her news of the hapless man.

"It's the same conspirators, including the King of Navarre and the Duc d'Alceon," he blushed and ducked his head in embarrassment, but Margot waved him on. "Mole gave up his accomplices, including Monsieur Coconnas," he nodded towards me and I nodded in understanding.

"Do they have evidence that they planned to kill my brother?" Margot gripped the table in front of her until her knuckles turned white. The young boy put his hands up, wordlessly. "So, it is simply an accusation," she concluded. There was hope for them, after all.

"Highness, it is the third conspiracy against the King in less than a year. I doubt that anything they say will make much of a difference."

"Then, I have to speak to my brother and mother." She pushed herself upright and was silent for a few moments. "Fetch me ink and paper!"

As soon as the boy was gone, I stood next to her, "What can you do, Margot? As he said, the conspiracies keep coming. What makes you think that the King won't simply execute all of them?"

She nodded, "We can't hope to save all of them, but we may save some of them."

"But is it worth the danger to you? Do you really want to save someone who stupidly plots against the King and his successor so much? They'll eventually lead you to prison, too."

She sat and rubbed her eyes, "Navarre can provide me a way out of court and I need to have a cordial relationship with at least one of my brothers. Charles won't last long," she crossed herself at the truth that we were all too afraid to speak aloud for fear of being accused of treason, "and I have no desire to ally myself with Anjou. He'll betray me at the first opportunity."

"Then, how do you save them both? *Can* you save them both?"

Margot spent the next day penning what would become a masterful response to the accusations against her husband and brother. Mole and Coconnas lingered in prison and we had little hope that either of them would feel the warmth of the sun again. Alceon threw himself on his Mother's mercy, giving up both men in order to save himself. The King would not easily pardon any of them this time and all of the conspirators were thrown into the prisons of Vincennes to await a special commission of five judges.

Alceon proved to be the spineless child that we all knew him to be, choosing to ramble on in front of the court, blaming his part of the conspiracy on a desire to escape to Flanders. Alceon claimed that the Dutch Protestants promised him governorship of Flanders, a charge that we all found laughable. Given how stupid Alceon had proven to be the previous year, it wasn't that difficult for the commission to believe that he was indeed that naive.

Alceon was not the only one who claimed an incredible amount of stupidity as his defense. Navarre rose to speak and pulled out a paper to read. The statement was extremely well crafted, because Navarre did not write it himself. He went on to claim that his escape attempts were necessary because the Valois had treated him so badly that he was all but compelled to escape. He had not been treated like a sovereign king and without her ruler, Navarre suffered greatly. Had the King and his mother treated him with the honor due his station, he added, he would be the King of France's most loyal vassal and potential ally.

The argument was typical of Margot, playing into the court's assumption that Navarre was a simpleton. It also pricked a sense of shame and guilt in the decision to hold another sovereign hostage, pricking the dying King's conscious. Margot's argument, delivered to the court in Navarre's voice, could not be refuted and both Navarre and Alceon escaped once again with their lives.

Still, the court would not let the incident pass without some form of punishment. While the princes were exonerated, someone must take the blame. The blame fell upon Mole and Coconnas, who under torture confessed to plotting the entire conspiracy. Once they accepted the blame, they were summarily sentenced to death.

"We have to do something!" Margot tapped her fingers on the book in her lap.

"You've managed to get two men off, so what can you do to help them?"

"I'll think of something, we have time before their execution." Both men were sentenced to a public beheading and time was very short if we were to save them.

"I will go to the King, he does love me." She dismissed me and I went back to my apartment. As I sat, I contemplated on what my life would be like without Coconnas. He was a balm in the ongoing fits of fear that plagued me. Where would I find that same easy companionship that I found with him?

While I mused, from the doorway, I heard Louis discreetly clearing his throat. Annoyed, I had no desire to listen to my husband's self-righteous lectures about my affair with Coconnas. "I am in no mood to hear it, Louis. I have a headache and I wish to be alone."

Ignoring me, he took several halting steps toward the bed where I sat. Wordlessly, he pulled out an envelope, edged with black. For a few moments, my mind could not make out the meaning of his motions. Then, before understanding could come, I immediately went into denial.

"I came to you as soon as I got the letter," his body shook and I saw the faintest trace of a tear fall down his cheek.

I said nothing, my head shaking. He proffered the envelope, as if my taking it would ease his own pain. I continued to shake my head, refusing to take it.

"It was yesterday. The doctor thought that he was fine, but--" A shaky inhalation cut off his words. If he said anything more, I did not hear it. I did not *want* to hear it.

I spent the next several days floating about like a wraith. Packing my things, I went directly to the Hotel de Nevers where I could have some semblance of privacy from the intrusive whisperings of the court. I allowed no one to see me, save a servant who placed a tray of food at my door. I honestly have no idea where my husband was in those dark days, since I cut myself away from all human contact. The world continued on, the trees outside my window budding with new blooms. I cared nothing for them, since my own life was stripped of color.

After about a week of my self-imposed isolation, my servant told me that I had a visitor, one who could not be refused. Before I could send either of them away, Margot appeared at my doorway. "There really is nothing that I can say to you that can help, I know that."

I stared at her, saying nothing. If I were not still numb, I would probably be touched at her show of compassion. My feelings were disconnected as a way to handle my devastation so I could only bite my lip in response.

"I've been an utter failure at espionage without you." She tried a wan smile, one that I could not return. . My humor would not return for weeks, if ever. Unsure at how to handle my mood, she pressed on.

"I tried to get Navarre and Alceon out of prison. I was going to visit them with one of my ladies. We would exchange clothing and have one of them walk out of the cell, pretending to be me. The guards never look under our masks or molest us to check our clothing. They wouldn't dare. By the time they did check, the men would be well out of Paris and we would be there to greet them."

"Margot, that idea is pathetic."

She shrugged, pleased to have gotten some response out of me. "I think it would have worked. Sadly, neither man could get together on who would pretend to be me."

"That was the weak point? Really, Margot—you are getting

terrible at plotting."

Another shrug, "I do better plotting with you."

I relented and allowed her to try to cheer me up until supper time, when she kissed my forehead and returned to her rooms at the palace.

By the end of April, the King was determined to remind all of France that its master and he stood firm in the decision to carry out the execution of La Mole and Coconnas on the last day of the month. Despite her continued pleas, Margot could not convince her brother to relent and spare our lovers.

The morning after their death, Margot came to my house and asked if I would do her a favor. As soon as she laid out her plan, I shook my head. "Margot, I don't think that it's wise," I tried to talk her out of the idea, but she stood firm.

"We'll do it under the cover of night, no one will see us. I can't live with the guilt."

Faced with sitting with my own grief or the distraction of Margot's misplaced romantic whimsy, I decided on the latter. As soon as the city was bathed in moonlight, we took an unmarked carriage to the place where the bodies of our lovers lay. "We should take their bodies and embalm them." She sounded so wistful that I felt sorry for her. My own son lay in the crypt at the cathedral of Nevers and I had been denied the opportunity to bury him during our hasty flight to Vincennes.

"Fine, but we can't possibly take their entire bodies with us. You have to be practical, Margot." I pleaded with her, feeling uneasy at the idea of what she had talked me into doing. To my relief, she nodded.

"Where can we put them?" Her look was pleading and I realized at that moment that she valued my opinion more than I realized. I also realized that she was more vulnerable than I had noticed before. Mole's death affected her more than I had initially assumed. "Somewhere out of the way." We talked to the driver, who suggested an unassuming out of the way chapel in the village of Montmare. The village was well out of Paris, and no one would think to look for their bodies there.

Thus, in a small, plain chapel in Montmare we had the heads of our lovers embalmed and perfumed. Margot insisted on this honor for both of them and she sobbed quietly as we had them both interred in the small space. For me, it became the service that I could not hold for my lost son whose body entered his tomb before I could see his face for the final time.

Exactly a month after Margot and I slipped out under the cover of darkness to bury the remains of our lovers, the entire country was in mourning. The King succumbed to tuberculosis, making the former Duc d'Anjou not just King of Poland but the new King of France. Margot was bereft as she detested her brother the new king. At the same time, my sister Marie was thrilled at the through of having her paramour returned to her.

"It's been misery having to be content with just words. I never realized how much I enjoyed his presence until I lost him." I could not help but feel pity for my sister; Conde had betrayed her and the King by escaping to Switzerland, reverting to Protestantism and declaring war upon the Valois. He had assembled an impressive number of Swiss mercenaries to fight for the Protestants against the new king. Marie was done with her husband and with the Queen Mother's help, actively petitioned the Vatican for an annulment. Once the King returned and the Pope granted her petition, I had no doubt that she would announce her plans to wed the king. First, however, she would have to endure the birth of her child.

Louis was also pleased to have the new King on his way to Paris. He would now become one of the closest advisors to the new monarch, much more important than he had been to the previous one. My husband spent so much time at the Louvre managing the transition between the rules that I rarely saw him. Louis had plenty of time to make the transition smooth, as the King spent the rest of the Summer dallying in his return to France. "It's due in part to that villain Conde," my sister Catherine told me one day. "He's amassing troops at the border and the King has to spend money he doesn't have in order to find soldiers to fight for him."

She glanced sidelong at me, "But I suppose Louis told you that already."

"He hasn't said anything to me. I don't remember the last time I spoke to him." I knew that I had embarrassed him and hurt his pride with my affair, but I did not care. My grief was so great that I had lost my ability to feel compassion for my husband.

"Guise has offered to raise an army for the King, but the Queen Mother doesn't trust him to shoe a horse these days." Catherine and I walked back from Mass, fanning ourselves in the relentless heat. With no King or Queen Consort to lead the court, we were left to our own devices that summer. Remaining united, Catherine and I kept a close watch over our younger sister and Catherine spent several days at the Hotel de Nevers hovering over Marie.

"If Louis were to offer to reconcile, would you do so?" Catherine's question hung in the air, and I mulled over the idea as we walked.

"I don't know." I really hadn't considered that option. I think that I had grown used to silence and awkwardness. Maybe I didn't want the burden of an active relationship with my own husband.

"Will you take another lover, then?"

I shook my head, surprised at my answer. "No, I still feel I lost Frederick because of him."

She rolled her eyes, "Oh, stop sounding like a pious Protestant! Frederick's death was not because you spent a few hours in some other man's bed. Feel guilt for being unfaithful if you wish, but not guilt over causing your child's death. Nothing I did caused the death of my daughter in December."

Catherine was probably right, but my lingering guilt kept me from agreeing with her. I could not stop the constant fear that I had caused Frederick's death with by betraying my marriage vows. I was terrified that I had caused the fraying of my own family, but I was also too terrified to confess those feelings to my sister.

By October, the new King finally arrived within the boundaries of France, staying in faraway Lyon. Louis left to meet him as soon as possible, as the court traveled to join up with the new sovereign. Not all of us went to Lyon, however, as Marie was so heavily pregnant that she could not make the long trip from Paris. Catherine and I volunteered to stay with her, and using Louis's absence as a pretext, I moved into the Hotel de Guise to help with the delivery of the child. Catherine was determined to repay Marie for her support in December and I was determined to stand with my sisters.

The time I spent with my sisters, reminded me of my own daughters, who would soon begin settling into the households of their future husbands. Although the tradition was generations old, I finally understood how difficult it was for a mother to send her child away from her. With Frederick gone, I would miss my remaining children more than I cared to admit. I had been so wrapped up in the permanent loss of my son to realize that the loss of my daughters would affect me just as deeply when the time came to give them up.

Marie's due date came and went, and impatient to be rid of any connection with Conde and greet the man she loved, Marie quickly grew agitated. "I'm so glad you're here—she's becoming impossible," Catherine complained to me one morning over breakfast.

"She's just as melodramatic as you are. Now I hope you can appreciate how difficult you can be."

She stopped in the middle of buttering a roll, "I am not difficult!"

"Catherine!" I put my knife down and glared at her. I was about to chastise her when we both heard a loud wail. Marie's labour had finally started.

The delivery was relatively quick and simple, although Marie was terrified throughout the ordeal. Thanks to God she gave birth to a girl, which meant that Conde would not move in to claim the child. Fate seemed to be smiling on my youngest sister finally.

The doctor would not hear of her leaving for Lyon before she had recovered and she reluctantly stayed abed for the next two weeks. Everything seemed to be going well and we started to make preparations for the King's return to Paris and my return to the Hotel de Nevers. I was glad for the opportunity to return to my daughters and for the time to be by ourselves before Louis returned. As I stood looking over my things, Catherine's young maid knocked on my chamber door.

"It's the Princess de Conde, My Lady." The young girl's face began to drain of color, terrifying me. I suddenly remembered the hours spent by Frederick's bed, weeping and praying for his recovery. In a daze, I ran behind her to see what I could do to help my youngest sister. At the doorway to Marie's chamber, Catherine stood talking to the doctor.

"It's a tear, Madame. We did not know about it until today when she started to decline."

"How long until she recovers?" They both met me with silence, terrifying me.

"It's bad," Catherine added, "she's lost a large amount of blood. Her maid found her moaning and there was a bloodstain already on the sheets."

"Then what's to be done?" I would not lose another family member, not this soon and not without any forewarning. God continued to be cruel with me for my single discretion.

"I've done all that I can do, I think prayer is needed more than anything. By all means, keep her calm."

Marie lingered on for almost two more weeks, continuously losing blood and slipping away from us. Between the three of us, she had always had the most delicate health. The stress of the birth combined with the shock of her husband's betrayal, sapped what little strength her slender body possessed. My sister had spirit and she held on by sheer will for as long as she could. Eventually, however, she slipped away from us before she could reunite with the King. Catherine sent word to the King in Lyon, whose grief was palatable. Guise wrote to her of how he prostrated himself in the loss of my sister. Together, Catherine and I awaited the return of the new King who would enter Paris behind two coffins.

Spring returned to Paris along with the court, a court much changed from the previous year. My sister would not preside over it as Queen Consort, which brought me much regret. Still, the King needed a wife and an heir, so he settled on a distant relative of the

Duc de Guise, a quiet girl named Louise, the daughter of the Duke de Mercoeur. As Louise was a Guise relation, the marriage sent the Queen Mother into a rage, claiming that the Guise were determined to regain power in France.

Most in the court called Louise "unremarkable," but to me, she was quite striking for her looks. Undoubtedly, she was beautiful, but that was not the issue. The new Queen bore a striking resemblance to my sister Marie. Henri III was determined to spend his life with my sister, going so far as to marry a woman who looked enough like her to cause me to catch my breath the first time I laid eyes upon her. Never at a loss for words, Catherine hissed into my ear afterwards, "Can you believe how much she looks like Marie! I never thought he really loved her, but if this isn't proof that he did, I don't know what is!" Louise's presence unnerved me and I resolved to stay as far away from her as possible, so as not to see my dead sister's presence in the new Queen's face.

The King had other plans, however. A week after his wedding, I was called to the Queen's Presence Chamber, where they sat on thrones. "Madame de Nevers, our beloved cousin. I have always enjoyed your loyalty and that of your husband." He inclined his head towards me and I curtsied.

"It would honor me and the Queen," he inclined his head towards her as she blushed mutely, "if you would serve as Her Majesty's Mistress of the Robes." Mistress of the Robes, the head of the Queen's household. The position was a great honor for anyone and if I were not so uncomfortable around the new Queen, I would be extremely honored at the position.

"Sire, I am unworthy. Yet, I feel that the Queen would feel uncomfortable with my presence given my relation with your Majesty..." the King cut me off before I could elaborate.

"That is why I need you to take on this honor. I will not have the Queen dishonored with talk that she is unworthy of her position. Your presence will signal to the court that her position is without question."

Thus, I was stuck without a way to refuse the appointment. Even more, I could not jeopardize Louis' standing with the king. As we did not currently have a male heir, I could not afford to insult the King. Wordlessly, I sank to my knees.

"Ah, wonderful!" The King clapped his head and I barely heard a "Thank you, Madame de Nevers" from the Queen's direction.

The practical aspects of managing the new Queen's household were not difficult for me. The massive numbers of maids, pages, ladies in waiting and demoiselles needed a leader, but the duties were not that more complicated than managing my own household. Many of the courtiers spent their lives in service to the royal family, so other than jostling for position, there was little I needed to do in order to keep the household in good order. What bothered me, was the constant reminder I would serve instead of a timid nobody picked from obscurity in Lorraine instead of my dead sister, Marie. Every time that I handled the Queen's jewels, I wondered what they would look like on Marie's neck. Each expensive brocade and silk the Queen chose for her gowns would have flattered Marie better. The court would have run better with my vivacious sister leading the activities. Yet, we were saddled with a mousy girl who spoke barely above a whisper and passively did everything that her husband told her to do.

The King was the Queen of the court in all but name, obsessively detailing complex etiquette rules that we all must adhere to and angrily fuming when we failed to do so. The formality was enough to give me a headache; and as much as possible, I avoided his presence. His brother's death raised Henri III to the throne and his arrogance raised him even further in his mind. Anyone else would be accused of putting on airs, but as he was the sovereign, no one could criticize him.

The Queen Mother was in a position to temper her son's arrogance, but as always, whatever Henri wanted, his mother smiled and obligingly agreed to. Unchecked, the King's ego grew larger, alienating the long-serving courtiers of France. The King rose to prominence a new crop of courtiers, an overwhelmingly male and attractive group that the court termed the "Mignons." The effeminate dandies, bolstered by the King's generosity and favor, did nothing to ingratiate themselves with us, making the divide between the old families and the new nobles even wider.

"He's becoming insufferable," I complained as Louis and I dined quietly together one evening in late Spring. I would never be stupid enough to say those words in front of anyone. Our marriage might have grown stale, but our partnership was as strong as ever.

He nodded, "He has no idea how much the court is beginning to hate him. He's less than a year on the throne and already the nobility is deserting him."

"And you?" The question and my fork hung in the air.

"I can't afford to desert him. You know that."

"Can you afford to alienate the rest of France?"

"The King commands the army; and I have no desire to place myself or this house at odds with the army."

"So, if you're forced to make a choice, you will back the King?"

"Yes, and as manager of the Queen's Household, *you* will have to make the same decision."

"Louis, France has been divided before, but each time before, it's fallen along lines of faith. Now, even the Catholics are making noise that they plan to desert him. When it's time to make that decision, what will you choose?"

He pushed his plate away from him. "The Catholics do not have a leader and the only backing they can ask from is from Spain. None of us want to be ruled by proxy by Spain."

"What if the Catholics become organized?"

"We'll simply have to make that decision if it presents itself. And," he looked directly at me, "we will make it together."

Louis' talk of us acting in solidarity served to lure me into a false sense of security. Assuming that any move we made would be made together, I paid little attention to my husband's business decisions as Summer dragged on. The King continued to show his contempt for the established noble houses, threatening the delicate balance of power we had created by generations of constant intermarriages. At the same time, the King grew bolder and more extravagant, wasting money that the country's treasury did not have on his favorites.

I would probably have remained ignorant of the goings on around me if I had not run into my father's agent in Flanders one day in the halls outside the Queen's audience chamber. "Monsieur Morel, I had no idea that you were in Paris." He gave me a quick bow in reply.

"I'm simply concluding the sale as per your husband's directions." I could not fathom what sale he referred to and at my confused look he hastened to add, "Your estate in Flanders. The Duc de Nevers was anxious that the funds be transferred to him as soon as possible."

"That's not possible—I have no desire to sell any of my lands in Flanders." I must have heard him wrong. The Flemish estates came directly from my father. They were amongst the ones that Catherine and I spent months arguing over. I refused to sell them in order to help alleviate the Guise's financial woes, despite the ongoing pressure from Guise. The idea that they could be gone was ludicrous. I had to sit down. In shock, I plunked gracelessly on a bench in the middle of the hallway.

"My Lady, I'm sorry. I was under the impression that you had authorized the sale of your lands. The Duc never gave me any indication that he--"

I put up a hand to stop him, "You have to cancel the sale."

His shoulders slumped. "I'm sorry, it's too late. The documents that I came to deliver to your husband are simply a legal formality."

My head swam as he continued to offer an apology. But Morel's words were not the ones that I wanted to here just then. I had to hear what my husband had to say.

"I have to speak to my husband, pardon me, Monsieur."

I rushed to the King's study, where Louis usually conducted his business. Usually, the room was occupied by my husband alone as the King preferred to leave the real business of running the country to his advisors. To my chagrin, there were several men in the room with their heads bent over one of the large tables in the study. I had no care for them and scattered them like the vultures that they were.

"Out! I will speak with my husband in private!" None of the men were stupid enough to argue with me, most likely because they saw the expression on my face. As soon as the last of them scurried out the room and closed the door, I turned upon my feckless husband.

"How dare you sell my lands in Flanders!" I spat out every word, boring my eyes into him. I waited for him to blanch or tremble, but my stoic husband never showed his emotions, even when his wife was in a murderous rage.

"The King asked me for a loan and it was the quickest way that I could secure the money."

"Oh, the King asked you for a loan and you immediately went out and started parceling out *my* lands in order to do his bidding? What a good little lap dog you are, Louis!" My voice dripped with venom, yet he did not so much as wince.

"Yes. The King himself asked me for something and I hastened to obey him. That is what I am expected to do as a loyal subject."

"Do not lecture me about loyalty, you who spent your time toadying up to whoever sat on the throne from the moment you came to France."

"You are calling me a whore, wife? I was not the one who spent his hours in another man's bed this year past." His words were a slap. I knew deep down that he held my infidelity over my head, ready to use it against me when the time came. Apparently, he thought that now was just that time.

Yet, I refused to take the bait. I was in the right and I was not about to let him cloud the argument with old sins. "Those lands are Cleves estates, handed down to me by my father. I am the mistress and I am the one to decide what happens to them."

"Yet, I am the Duc de Nevers and it is my decision that the law honored."

I walked until I was mere inches away from his face. "You are the Duc only by the King's command. You have what you have today because of *me*."

"I have what I have today because the King allowed a woman to inherit. That came from the King's benevolence. Without it, the lands would go to the Guise." He slyly reminded me of our lack of a male heir. This only reopened an old wound. I had still refused to forgive him for keeping me from Frederick. The anger seethed inside me like a tempest.

"You, yourself, told me that we were to remain united in our decisions, but at the first opportunity, you betray me and sell my inheritance. Remember that I am a Bourbon, a cousin of the King and that the Guise can just as easily back me as they could back you. Are you ignorant enough to make an enemy of your own wife?"

"I am not ignorant enough to make an enemy of the King. My wife's anger I can deal with, the King's wrath I cannot."

"Remember your decision today. Today, I learned how easily you will choose Henri Valois over me." I stalked out of the library and past the chastened men who loitered awkwardly outside of the room.

"There really is no telling just what my brother will use the money for. He may plan to go to war, or he may want gold thread for a coat for that snake Du Gaust." She spat out the name, reminding me that Du Gaust had become her most potent enemy at court. United in our anger, Margot and I fumed over the deal struck between Louis and the King. I thanked God for her loyalty. Unlike my husband, I could always trust Margot to stand beside me and never betray me.

"Louis has plenty of estates from his grandmother that he could sell, the nerve of him to take my lands!" As we spoke, I glanced around the banquet hall to see that Madame de Sauve was feeding bread suggestively to the Duc d'Alceon, who now was also the new Duc d'Anjou thanks to his brother's largess.

"I have to ask you a favor and the best part is that it will put Madame de Sauve's nose quite out of joint." Margot smiled and wiggled her eyebrows suggestively.

"Margot, I'm trying to talk to you about something serious, and you're scheming?" Despite her reputation for frivolity, Margot usually knew the line of propriety and rarely violated it in her public behavior.

"This is serious," she moved her lips to my ear so that only I could hear. A couple of men saw the gesture and raised their tankards towards us, misinterpreting it as a sexual advance. "Alceon finally has a plan in place to escape and get to the Netherlands."

"Come on, Margot—every attempt that he's made so far has been a bumbling failure."

"This time, he has a plan, financial backing, an escape route and help along the route. All he needs is a plausible cover story."

"Why should I go along with this?"

"Once it happens, your husband will be humiliated and Madame de Sauve's stock with my mother will go down precipitously."

Spite caused my interest to spike at her words. "Tell me about it."

"Well, we'll need to start touring monasteries."

Margot had a cover story; I was going to pray for the soul of my son and she was going to seek absolution for her sinful ways. Really, the idea of us touring monasteries was absurd and I was convinced that the King and his mother would object as soon as they heard it. I was wrong; they both found the idea of Margot seeking absolution so absurd that neither of them suspected that we were up to no good.

Early on the morning of September 15th, we penitents set out for our tour of the monasteries and religious houses on the outskirts of Paris in my own coach. During lunch, one of Margot's demoiselles complained of nausea and began to vomit. "Take her back to the Louvre," Margot signaled the guards assigned to accompany us for the day. At the Saint-Honore gate of the palace, the poor girl signaled the coachman that he must stop so that she could get fresh air. Moments later, she got back into the coach and in a strained voice pronounced herself fit to return to the monastery. Unwilling to put himself in trouble with the Queen of Navarre, the coachman simply obeyed her instructions and turned away from the gates of the palace.

At the monastery, the girl scurried away while the coachman and the guards loitered. Unbeknownst to any of them, the "girl" was the Duc d'Alceon, who used the lack of care to slip away on the grounds of the monastery in my coach and onto safety. Margot's current lover, a young gallant named Du Bussy, conveniently left him a horse that he used to ride away to safety.

Despite the ludicrous nature of the plan, we had helped Alceon to finally make his escape. With the prince gone, the King had a voice of dissension, one that was far away from the continual surveillance of the court. And for the King, the idea was dangerous.

Realizing that he had a conspiracy unfolding under his own nose, the King sent his most trusted soldiers out to fetch his missing brother. The detachment was headed by none other than my own husband. Unsure of who to trust, the King knew that Louis had demonstrated his loyalty. Margot and I continued to loiter at the monastery, talking at length with the abbot about religious issues. Before supper, the guard led by my husband realized that the Duc made his escape via my coach and we heard a rumbling sound before the doors of the abbey.

"My Lord—how may we help you this evening?" The lanky abbot greeted Louis as he sat astride his horse.

"The King's brother is missing and we have reason to believe that he stole my wife's coach in order to make his escape." Louis looked around the courtyard, as if Alceon would suddenly appear from behind a bush.

One of the priests came to fetch Margot and I, clearing his throat as we sat nonchalantly with the abbot. "Madame, the Duc de Nevers is at the gate. He says that the Duchess's coach is missing."

I rolled my eyes melodramatically. "That's impossible. I set it to the Louvre to deposit one of the Queen's demoiselles. It's probably in the stables as we speak. My husband must be having trouble with his eyesight."

"The Duc seems convinced that it is missing," he shuffled his feet and spread his hands helplessly.

"Well, let's see what Louis is all about, shall we?" Margot rose to her feet, causing the rest of our party to stand. She swept gracefully out of the room and soon we stood at the door of the monastery.

"Louis, what on earth is all of this commotion?" I glanced at the assembled men and horses, careful to show my annoyance at the disturbance.

"The Duc d'Alceon is missing and we have reason to believe that he used your carriage to make his escape."

"The coach is probably right where he should be," Margot adopted the same haughty stance and she folded her arms. "My demoiselle has returned, so the coach should be in the stables of the monastery. Go send someone to check." The delay was timed to ensure that wherever Alceon was, he had more than enough time to make his escape. The longer we kept Louis standing still, the more time we bought for Alceon. Margot and I would stall for all that we were worth.

Margot inspected the trim at the cuff of her dress while we continued to stall for time. "The Duchess' coach is missing, My Lord." At his words, I changed tactics.

"Where is the demoiselle we sent to the Louvre? Merciful Lord, has something happened to her?" I crossed myself piously, causing the assembled group to do the same. If I distracted them with worry over the girl, perhaps they would delay even longer.

"The girl has been accounted for, wife. It is the coach that is still missing." Louis's jaw was clenched tightly. He was likely on to my ruse, but Margot and I would play the assembled crowds for as long as we could. Perhaps we could be the first players in the acting troupe that Margot considered founding.

"Praise God she is safe." At Margot's words, I nodded.

"And you think that the Duc himself took my carriage?" I posed the question to one of the men, knowing that by ignoring Louis, I was further enraging him.

"Without a way to get home, we'll have to find another way back to Paris." Margot was as adept as anyone in delaying tactics and she put her skills to good use.

"Majesty, you may stay in some of the monks' rooms, although, I doubt that they will be up to the standards that you ladies' are used to." The monks were more than willing to see to our comfort, especially if it meant a sizable donation from Margot and myself.

While she inclined her head in thanks, Louis's horse stamped impatiently.

"Then now, that is settled, I must be off to find your coach, wife. We'll send another one for the two of you tomorrow morning." At that, he spurred his mount and the detachment followed. As soon as they were out of earshot, Margot turned to me. "Well, that went well, I think."

The next morning, the guardsmen that had been sent to guard the coach lent to us told us that Louis had located my coach ten miles outside of Paris. Apparently, the occupant leapt from the carriage and onto a waiting horse. Alceon had made his escape and the King had an unaccounted for rival speeding towards the Netherlands. If Alceon were to meet up with Conde's Protestant forces, the King would have another civil war, this one fought against his own brother and heir.

Margot and I kept up the ruse that my coach was stolen while under a mission of mercy for an ailing demoiselle. If the King suspected Margot and I had a hand in the plot to get Alceon away, I never heard any remonstration from him. If anything, I think that the King believed that I was as loyal as my husband.

Louis, however, knew better. He met me in the large salon of our home as I watched the September sun set before me. Although I could hear and sense his presence in the room, I did not bother to turn to greet him. Instead, I kept my gaze at the sunset as the orange sun set slowly.

"I told you not to make an enemy of me, Louis."

"I told you not to make an enemy of the King."

"Then, I believe that we are at a standstill." I clasped my hands behind my back and finally turned to look at him. Rather than enraged, he looked tired.

"There was no damage to your carriage or your horses. Apparently, the royal thief treated them quite well."

"Then, I have to thank him for that. Most thieves are not so generous."

"Henriette, this is not time for us to be at odds. We are more vulnerable than ever."

"If you truly believed that, then why do something so underhanded? Something that you knew would make me angry?"

"I had no choice. The King constantly abandons the men who helped him to the throne for those fawning flops. If I am not careful, then I will find myself on the outside as well."

"So, you do everything to keep the King's favor?

"At one time, so would you." The words were truer than I wanted to admit. But we had lost far too much between the time in which we were united in our goals and that quiet September evening.

"Am I to be forgiven for Frederick?"

"I don't know." I honestly did not know if I could *ever* forgive him. He had made too many stupid decisions in an attempt to appease the new King, not the least of which was sacrificing part of my inheritance. How foolish would my husband's next decision be? Could I count on him to look after both of our interests? Could I even *trust* him?

"I need time, Louis." It was all I could give him.

The next morning, while on an errand for the Queen, I walked into Margot's apartments to find her gripped with terror. "He'll come for me! I shouldn't have done this! What was I thinking, I know him too well!" It was such an abrupt change from the day before that I started to wonder if Margot had gone mad.

"What is the matter? You were fine when I left." I quickly sent word to Queen Louise that the Queen of Navarre had taken ill and gently sat Margot down on her bed.

"I have to stay here. It's the only safe place that's left." Margot began to speak nonsense and her face went white. She tore at the laces in her gown and I worked to loosen it to allow her to breathe.

"Start from the beginning, did someone threaten you?"

"Henri. He'll torment me. He always does. And my Mother will let him do it. He'll beat me and I won't live to see the next morning." At that, she began crying like a little child and I finally understood the cause of her terror. Anjou had terrorized her since childhood and with the crown of France sitting on his over-indulged head, there was no limit to how he would punish Margot for Alceon's disappearance. She truly was safer in a sickbed. I began making preparations to place her in bed and sent word via her page that she was not to be disturbed. I would do all that I could to protect Margot from her brother's unbridled rage.

As I sat beside her, murmuring words of comfort, I began to realize that a sickbed might be the one place where I was safe as well. Without his sister to take the brunt of his frustration, the King might take his anger out on me. Like two cowards, we hid in Margot's bedchamber and waited out the repercussions of Alceon's escape.

Two days into our ruse, Louis came to Margot's chamber and asked to speak with me. Grabbing me about the waist, he pulled me against his body and whispered in my ear. "Make no motion to startle her. Listen closely to what I say." At his words, my blood ran cold, but I simply nodded.

"The demoiselle you sent to Paris in your coach? The king ordered her drowned to make an example of her. If a group of boatmen hadn't rescued her in time, she would be floating in the Seine right now." The horror of the lengths to which the King would go to avenge himself appalled me.

"Louis, you have to believe now that appeasing him is pointless."

He gave a short sigh, unwilling to concede my point. "We don't have much of a choice. Keep a close eye on Du Gaust, he's the one who helped the King plan this abomination." Du Gaust, the man who Margot had marked as her enemy. If he was willing to plot a punishment on Margot's proxy, what would he have in store for Margot? How safe was *I*?

I did not argue when Louis insisted that I go home with him that night. He did not argue when I insisted that I did not feel safe without him hovering over me. In fact, I began to demand that my husband sleep beside me for weeks afterwards in the hope that if Du Gaust came for me, I might have his protection. Our reconciliation, even one born out of fear of my life, came at a fortuitous time. By the New Year, I learned that I was once again pregnant.

Navarre also made his escape and this time, neither Margot nor I aided him in doing so. Margot learned of his escape from the Queen Mother and the King was so incensed that my friend was enclosed in her rooms pending the King's pleasure.

"Louis, I have to see her. She'll think that I've abandoned her."

He shook his head, "Think of how angry the King was in September and increase that anger exponentially. I will not have you at risk for assassination this time." I opened my mouth to argue with him, but he cut me off, "Please, Henriette—I am doing this for your safety." I was miserable without Margot and I spent most of my time in the Queen Louise's presence, sulking and trying to hide the fact that I was sulking. "Madame de Nevers, are you all right?" Louise looked at me with genuine concern, and I felt guilt for my behavior.

"I'm pregnant again, Your Majesty. The nausea is too much for me. Please forgive me, it will go away in a month or two." I gave her a weak smile, hoping that she would accept my excuse.

"Of course, and God bless you for your miracle. I will pray for you." I felt a momentary stab of guilt at blurting out my news. Since the day of her wedding, the King and Queen worked to conceive an heir and I realized that my widening stomach would only serve to rub her failure in her face. Perhaps if I were a younger woman, I would smugly rub the situation in her face. Having lost a beloved child, however, I knew firsthand that children were not trophies to be held over the head of a less fortunate woman.

Thanks to my position as Mistress of the Robes, I had secured a position for my sister Catherine as a senior lady in waiting, which meant that the two of us were able to spend more time together. With the loss of Margot, I cherished the opportunity to be with my sister all the more. Catherine, for her part, cherished the opportunity to gossip with me. "The Queen Mother charged Madame de Sauve with estranging Alceon, Navarre and Margot from one another."

I need not ask why, but my curiosity was piqued as to how. Catherine was more than willing to provide the details, as far as she knew them. "Navarre is convinced that the Protestants would not support Alceon intaking the Netherlands unless he came to lead them in person. That's why he was so eager to leave court this time." She quickly glanced around the room to see if anyone else was listening in. "Madame de Sauve gave Navarre a note supposedly from Margot to her latest lover asking him to slit Navarre's throat if he so much as tarried from Mass. I doubt he'll try to make an escape. He certainly isn't bothering to speak to Margot."

"That doesn't sound like Margot at all," I pulled my face into a grimace. "She risked her life to save him after their wedding and when Mole and Coconnas were executed. Why on earth would she bother to work against him now?"

She shrugged, "Maybe the letter is a fake. No one knows for sure, but Navarre certainly took it to heart. Word is that he's too scared to even join the King for a hunt." The three were barely speaking to one another at the moment and Margot's isolation from the two men made it easier for the King to forgive his sister, at least momentarily. With a temporary truce between the King and his sister, Margot left her gilded prison a few weeks later.

If Navarre was gullible enough to believe the threats on his life, he soon regained his taste for the hunt. One cold February morning, goaded by Guise into participating in the hunt or risking his masculinity forever, he relented and took off for the forest surrounding Fountainbleu with the King and Guise. Lured into a false sense that Navarre was too terrified to leave the party, Guise and the King stalked off from him and were soon too involved in running the stag down before they realized that their royal party was one person short. Navarre had given the King the slip after all. Margot need not feign innocence at Navarre's escape; the King and Queen Mother had no doubts that she was left in the dark during this most recent plot. Virtually the moment Navarre returned to his own kingdom, he recanted Catholicism and once again became a Protestant. Still, they could not let the loss of both hostages go and Margot remained isolated from the court. Months passed until the King realized that his support amongst the nobility was so eroded that he could not risk further alienating his younger siblings.

Louis bent over his papers as we finished our supper. "We're about to be hit with a large tax and there isn't anything that I can do to stop it." At the mention of money, my head snapped up and I dropped the crust of bread in my hand.

"How much does he expect from us now?" My anger boiled within me. If Louis planned on selling any of our properties to pay this new tax, he would bear the brunt of my anger. The past two years had been uneventful, which gave us time to repair our marriage. I had once again grown to trust that my husband would consult me in any decisions that affected both of us.

"Substantial. Villequier convinced him that since the royal treasury is virtually empty, the noble families that are now too wealthy will have to make up for the shortfall." Louis detested Villequier, one of the King's minions elevated to chamberlain and given the duty of "advising" the king alongside him. With the minions isolating the King, he heeded less and less of Louis's advice.

"I suppose the King is unaware that the missing money is due to the gifts to his minions and those extravagant pageants we have to attend every night?" Determined to keep up appearances, despite the angry court and a continued lack of heir, the King distracted himself with squandering more money than his elder brother ever had. "And the Parlement can do nothing to stop or at least delay this madness?"

Louis shook his head. "Today, the King personally walked into the Parlement of Paris and laid the edict down in front of them. Before any of them could so much as discuss it, he turned his back on them and walked away. There is no protest in Parlement and the King's determined to keep them securely under his thumb."

"So, he brings us all to the brink of bankruptcy while we are denied the opportunity to check his power?" The endless rounds of evening activities were wearing thin on me. It was 1578, the King had only been on the throne for less than four years and already he had managed to alienate all but the most toadying of his supporters. No matter how much the Queen Mother tried to avoid an oncoming disaster, he pushed us towards it.

I had no desire to stand wildly by while the Mignons ran wild as bucks throughout the palaces, willfully compromising the virtue of the Queen's ladies and making a mockery of the Crown. Queen Louise was in no position to speak to her husband, intimidated by him as she was. She left all of the awkward confrontations involved in running her household to me. I spent virtually every day engaged in arguments with courtiers and creditors in the Queen's name. With a toddler waiting for me at home, I was in no mood to mother a grown woman with no backbone.

The toddler in question ran into the dining room, in a childish imitation of the horseplay I witnessed from the Mignons during the day. On a rosy-cheeked two-year-old, it was endearing. "Papa! Papa!" Francis ran to Louis and beat on his shins, demanding that he take him in his arms. Louis wasted no time in scooping him up in his arms and covering his face with kisses. "Son, I must teach you gentlemanly behavior, I fear the men at court are poor role models."

I smiled, knowing that he had no plans whatsoever to seriously chastise our son. After years spent criticizing Catherine de Medici for overindulging her son who now sat on the throne of France, I now began to understand why she did so. Neither Louis nor I were willing to do anything that would crush the boy's spirit. Unlike our dear Frederick, Francis was fat and robust almost from the moment of his birth. We both carried a superstitious fear that if we did anything to break his healthy spirit, we would also damage his body. God had given us a second chance with this child and we were determined to do nothing to endanger him.

"Do you want to put him to bed?" Louis tickled him under his chin and he giggled in return. I shook my head. Francis often made a game of running to one of us and demanding attention. As the nurse trailed behind our son, I watched as Louis took him to his bedroom. Before I settled down for the night, I wanted to catch up on my correspondence. Very soon, letters would be all that I had of Margot. Navarre sent word that he wanted his wife to join him in his own kingdom and jumping at the chance for freedom from her brother, she agreed. Led by Margot and her mother, most of the court would depart for a tediously long trip across France to Navarre.

As head of Queen Louise's household, I could not go. Neither the King or his consort would join the rest of the court to Navarre. I selfishly wanted my friend to stay with me in Paris and if it weren't for the need to watch over Francis, I would have begged Louis and the King to go with her as far as the border. "It's best that you stay in Paris," Louis confided to me one night as we lay in bed. "Margot and the Queen Mother are traveling to the most divided parts of France. There are declared Protestant towns that will not allow Catherine to even enter and Margot's dowry lands will not allow that heretic Navarre to set foot in them." Undeterred, Catherine gathered her Flying Squadron to entice the humorless men of the Navarrese court into their beds. Chief amongst them was Madame de Sauve, who Catherine dispatched to ensnare Navarre again in a haze of nostalgia.

Thus, deprived of the people who usually made court bearable, I was forced to endure the Mignons without any buffer between us. Even Claude Catherine had departed Paris to take care of her husband's country estates. The King grew even more erratic, spending more time in selecting the dogs he and the Queen took in their daily walks than running the affairs of the kingdom. The dogs became a point of contention between myself and the Queen. In order to escape being molested by the unchecked Mignons, many young demoiselles ran from them and into the relative safety of Louise's apartments. Eventually, we became a sort of asylum for girls who had no desire to lose their virtue to the Mignons, which meant, I had to find space for them out of sight of the men of the King's inner circle.

At the same time, the King could not be dissuaded from bringing more and more lap dogs into the Queen's apartments. The animals regularly exceeded a dozen flea-bitten and raucous animals. As soon as I managed to quiet the fearful young girls and the yapping beasts, the King would appear to rile up the latter. As always, no one could make the King see reason and the Queen was completely incapable of taking a stand against her husband. The Queen Mother was my only hope for speaking to the King, but with her departure to Navarre, I could not count on her support.

"Louis, perhaps I should resign my position?" As he entered our bedchamber, I noticed that he beamed with the time he spent with Francis.

He sighed, "I'm sorry—I know it's insufferable. But with the King's favorites blocking the way to him, I can't afford to lose any influence within the court."

An idea suddenly came to me. "Perhaps I should leave with Catherine to meet her husband's family." Our eldest daughter was now ten and old enough to join the household of her betrothed, the eldest son of the Duc de Longueville. It would mean leaving her seven-year-old sister, Marie and Francis in Paris with Louis. We had the eldest son of the Duc de Mayenne in mind for Marie, but we still had years before she would also need to leave us for the large nursery at Joinville.

"I doubt that the King or the Queen would fault you for seeing that our daughter is settled in. Speak to Louise and see if she agrees to it."

As it turned out, Louise was very eager for me to depart for her family's own lands. "Madame de Nevers, if you would, I would like to send these letters to my sister." She produced a stack of letters from her bureau. As I tucked the letters into my cape, I heard an earthly screech from behind me. Louise jumped and fearing the worst, I turned to see if we were being invaded by some unholy demon. To my horror, I saw that we were not that lucky.

On his shoulder, the King carried an animal that looked like an upright dog. I managed to bite my tongue before I asked what manner of animal would join the court this time. "Look, Madame —our ambassador of Venice has gifted us with a monkey!" A smile split across his face and I felt cold horror creep up from my stomach to my head. My escape from the insanity of the court would happen just in time.

"Mama, what will my husband be like?" I looked down at

Catherine, who unfortunately shared my frizzy blonde hair. Knowing firsthand how difficult it was to keep those curls under control, I had given my maid, Lydia, the only woman who could handle my own hair, as a gift to my daughter. We had traveled for days in our coach and I relished the opportunity to pay childish games with her for the last time. We were accompanied only by Lydia and the girls who would wait upon my daughter. Usually, we would gather a large retinue to demonstrate our importance and that of her husband-to-be's family, but I wanted to enjoy peace and intimacy with my eldest child as long as possible.

"He will be very kind and he will love you very much." My daughter solemnly asked the question, but I did not want to sully the day with talk of reality. Both of my daughters would marry powerful Dukes, ones who would protect them when Louis and I could not. Francis would inherit our lands, but our daughters would be placed in wealthy households where they would want for nothing. .

"Will he be handsome?" She persisted and for a second, I thought of my sister Marie.

"All men are handsome in their own way. It is your duty as a wife to bring out his handsomeness and his piety." Her namesake had been married to her first husband at twelve, only two years older than my daughter was now. I could not imagine how Catherine stood the pressure of becoming a bride at such a tender age. I made a note that when I returned to Paris, I would try to be more compassionate towards my remaining sister.

Days after I returned to Paris, I realized that I was once again pregnant. Louis did nothing to hide his pleasure at the idea of our having another child. With Francis constantly tugging at my skirts, I grew larger as we awaited the birth of our latest child. We had our heir and two beautiful daughters who would marry well and settle in great noble houses. This most recent child almost seemed a bonus for us.

In April of 1580, my labor began and ten hours later, the midwife announced that we had another son. I heard a joyful whoop from the hallway as the midwife told Louis of the news. Once we were recovered, my husband all but danced into our bedchamber to inspect the new baby. "This is completely unexpected, yet totally wondrous." Uninterested in either of us, our new son let out a long yawn and closed his eyes and began to sleep. We named the boy Charles and began to enjoy the security of having two sons in our nursery.

On the heels of our joy, we experienced once again the greatest loss that anyone can endure. In June, the nurse took Francis outside to play in the warm sunlight. Newly returned to my post in the Queen's household, I joined the court at the chateau of Blois in the Loire Valley. Lost in my thoughts, I did not hear Louis as he rushed into the Queen's Presence chamber, or Louise's acknowledgement of his presence.

"Henriette-" he could only choke out my name. Hearing the anguish in his voice, I turned to look at him. Forgetting the strict layers of etiquette the King enforced at court, Louis dissolved into tears and one of the Queen's matrons grabbed him. He continued to sob for over ten minutes as the sense of horror spread across the room. "I've just received word. Francis was playing and he fell, and--" he once again succumbed to his sobs and the matron held him as if she were his own mother. I stood alone in the room, seeing nothing. At my side, the Queen embraced me and held me as I sobbed. After the years I spent criticizing her for the sin of not being my sister, the young woman took this opportunity to show me the greatest compassion when I needed it.

Louise continued to show me the kind of support and generosity that I had never thought the quiet woman capable of. She immediately had Masses said for Francis and she insisted that I take time in my chambers to mourn my son. Adding to her kindness, when Louis and I left Blois for Nevers to inter Francis's tiny body, the Queen absolutely insisted that we take her own coach. In the midst of my overwhelming grief, I came to the realization that France had a Queen worthy of the title after all.

In the months following Francis's death, the Queen remained firm in her insistence that I reduce my duties and concentrate on my remaining children. Unfortunately, I did just that, hovering over Marie and Charles constantly. Less than an hour after I returned to court, my sister Catherine marched in and began ordering me about as if she were our mother. She proved to be the perfect replacement for Margot, who stubbornly remained in Navarre to head its court, while constantly arguing with her husband.

After Margot's departure, almost three years earlier, our salons with the Duchess de Retz were gone, which dismayed my friend Claude Catherine to no small end. "We really need to gather up what we have left and have a go of it. We need a party and *you* need one in particular." She locked arms with me one morning as we all filed out from daily Mass.

I shook my head, "I don't have time for that nonsense. Marie and Charles need me. What if something happened to them and I wasn't there?" Claude turned to me, exasperated. "Henriette, I will tell you something that no one will and it is for your own good. There is good parenting and there is obsession. You have reached the point of obsession." A gust of wind flew past us and we turned to see the source. It turned out to be my over-sized brother-in-law, the Duc de Guise. His face was mottled with red and his jaw set so hard, I wondered if he might break it. "Brother, are you alright?"

"It is the King," he said no more, but I knew that there was much more. The King had marked his old playmate Guise as his whipping boy two years earlier when one of the Mignons died in a fight with one of Guise's retainers. Given how many fights the Mignons were involved in, I don't know why this one bothered the King so much. Yet, when Guise shielded his man from punishment in the duel, the King was livid. .

The Guise and their Lorraine kin were too well placed in the governing of France, beginning with my mistress, the Queen. The King could not risk dismissing them all without courting open rebellion. So, Henri did the next best thing, causing grief for my sister and her giant of a husband. While most of the court managed to hide our contempt for the king and his gang of criminals, Catherine and Guise openly showed their disgust of the King and his rule. For his part, the King humiliated the Guise clan in small ways that began to add up over the years. Eventually, the Guise would not stand for the constant slights to their honor and would find ways to get revenge on the King.

"Catherine told me that she's tried to enlist the Queen Mother's help in speaking with the King, but it's as if she's virtually retired. I'm sorry, I know how annoying those villains can be."

Guise's greatest strength lay in his affability, "Thank you, Sister. I keep thinking that the King will one day go too far and his mother will have to step in and curb his excesses. Sadly, that day seems very far off."

"At least Catherine is safe in Louise's retinue," Claude piped up beside me. Guise turned to give her a courtly bow. The Queen remained neutral, generous to her Guise cousins and her royal husband. In fact, Louise's chambers might well have been the most neutral location in all of France.

"And I have to spend each day in the King's presence, which is wearing quite heavily on my patience. If you will excuse me, Ladies." He gave us a gracious smile and swept down the hall.

From that moment on, I made an effort to observe the irritation level of my sister and her husband. Louis and I could afford to take a neutral stance, which would benefit us as the gulf between the King and the Guise continued to widen. At court festivities, I kept an eye on the interactions between the two men, always taking mental notes.

One day, as I sat with the Queen, the King strode into her inner chambers and sat talking with the ladies. As the Queen and the rest of the assembled group chatted, the King took my arm and pulled me to a private corner. "Madame de Nevers, I must ask a favor of you."

"Of course, Majesty." The previous "favor" involved the king sending a litter of puppies to Catherine and Charles, so I expected this latest one would be just as harmless.

"I have reason to believe that one of my friends is playing false with me and trying to tempt the Queen." This did have something to do with me; if the Queen's honor was in danger of being besmirched, it was my duty to protect it. Given how much generosity she had shown the past year, I was more than willing to repay her for her compassion towards me.

"Are you sure?" I snuck a quick glance at the Queen, who looked as innocent as ever. The King nodded his head slowly, looking forlorn.

"But, surely you can punish the man or banish him?"

"Sadly, no. But, I believe that you can save your mistress' honor much easier than I can. I think that this man is an adventurer. An affair with one woman at court is the same as an affair with another…"

His words had me confused, "You want me to pick out a woman to carry on an affair with this man?"

"I want you to lure him into an affair with *you*. Now, hear me out, Cousin," he used a term that he always used when he wanted something difficult from me. "I have no desire to make you unfaithful to your husband. I only want you to carry on the facade of an affair."

"And I suppose Louis is to know of this?"

He nodded, "Certainly. I will tell Louis of this great favor that you are doing for me. He will know that you are true to him." He once again adopted a forlorn look. The King had certainly thought this charade out well. With horror, I began to wonder if this was the game that he played with my sister years earlier. Had I been terribly wrong then and he had never loved Marie? Did I unwittingly assist him in using my sister for his own sick games against Conde? The thought sickened me. I had to get to Louis to talk to get his opinion about this. At the same time, I could not risk alienating the King by refusing his request. I was trapped like a fly in his schemes. I had to delay him.

"Sire, I will speak with Louis to ensure that we are united in this plan. I have no desire to embarrass my husband in front of the entire court."

He nodded, "Of course. Say nothing to anyone of this plan, especially the Queen. I promise that in doing this, you will be richly rewarded. As always, you have my thanks for your service to my gentle wife." He kissed my hand and walked away from me. Within seconds, he rejoined the women surrounding his wife and kissed her lovingly on the cheek.

"What do you want me to do? Honestly, Louis—I will do nothing without your complete blessing." Determined not to hurt my husband and having no desire whatsoever to be unfaithful to him, I would follow along with whatever he decided to do. We had long since moved past our earlier problems in our marriage and he had proven true to his word to make no more decisions without consulting me. We were once again united as a team.

"There really is no way that you can say no to this scheme." Louis shook his head, the realization that the King was becoming more and more unmanageable sinking in. "I insist that any correspondence you have with that man, I see it."

"See it? My love, you are going to compose it with me. I have no desire to walk into this without you." We sat at the table in his study and I reached across to grasp his hand. He squeezed it gently and smiled at me.

"Very well, that settles your written communication. What will you do when you see him in person?"

I hated to raise the specter, but the truth was that I had the answer in front of me. "I'll carry on as the King did with Marie. I will claim that I am assailed with doubts and that I cannot for the foreseeable future consummate our affair. With any luck, by then, the King will have all of the proof he claims he needs and I'll be released from this Devil's bargain."

"The air is quite sweet this evening." I slipped close to Monsieur de Levas, the Mignon the King asked me to seduce. I suddenly began to understand the level of anxiety Madame de Sauve and her compatriots felt when spying for the Queen Mother. Hopefully, I would be as successful as de Sauve.

"I think that it's the company, especially the ladies." With his arms folded, Levas leaned against a pillar of the ballroom of

Fontainebleau. Given how cavernous the room was, it was easy for me to position myself beside him without drawing too much attention from the crowd.

"You do seem to be enjoying yourself." I hadn't used my flirtation skills for a while, but I could manage light banter with anyone. Luckily, he continued to take my bait.

"The court is always a place where I feel welcome." He turned to me with a heated expression. I was instantly ill at ease. The double entendre was not lost on me at all. He was more aggressive than I had assumed. I would have to be on my guard to keep him in bay.

"Tell me, Sir—what duties do you do for the King?" On the surface, it was a safe topic, but given the incessant rumors that some of these dandies spent their nights in the King's bed, perhaps it was not.

"Well, His Majesty has asked me to coordinate the training of our troops in Normandy. The Duc de Joyeuse recommended me. Of course, we are great friends and I would be glad to aid him in the endeavor." Good God, not only was the man vapid and arrogant, he was determined to take any political appointment that he could steal from experienced men. Maybe Guise was right after all. I wanted nothing more than to get away from this blowhard, but I had to remain near him in order to complete my mission.

"Will you have to depart for Normandy soon?" With any luck, he would do so and the supposed threat to the Queen's honor would be gone with him.

"Probably in two weeks, I will be sad to leave Paris." He sighed and fondled the tapestry behind him as if it were a woman's body. The action made my skin crawl. His crassness also made me wonder if the man might well be stupid. There would be few verbal jousts between us, unlike Coconnas.

"If you would like, I could write to you Madame de Nevers. The hardships of war are always lightened by letters from a beautiful woman."

"I would love to do that!" I turned to him and tried to adopt the breathless behavior of the demoiselles who flirted constantly at the court.

"Then, I await word from you." He kissed my hand, as he did so, I noticed that he took care to glance in Louis' direction.

Aided quite capably by Louis, I sent regular letters to Normandy, telling Levas how his presence caused my heart to flutter. Sometimes, I thought that the verbiage was overwrought, but Louis would giggle at the naughtiness. A steady stream of letters came from Normandy, most with passages that made me blush. I had Louis read each of them aloud and he often used a falsetto as he read Levas' words to me.

At the same time, I kept a close watch over the letters that came to the Queen. As her chief Lady in Waiting, one of my tasks was to manage the Queen's correspondence. I was relieved to see that there were no letters from Normandy, not even from some of the Queen's Lorraine cousins. I suppose that she could have enlisted another lady to carry her letters to Levas, but that did not sound like Louise at all. As always, the Queen seemed to be irreproachable in her behavior.

Months after our supposedly clandestine correspondence began, I sat with Claude at the banquet given by the King for the court to celebrate the end of the long Summer. Claude continued to try and enlist my help in reviving our salons, but without Margot's presence, they seemed almost pointless. "After this banquet is over, I plan to go to bed and sleep for hours." Popping a grape into my mouth, I stared at Claude with a mock—threatening expression.

She burst into laughter at me. "Henriette, you have become the worst type of woman: a boring one!" I joined her in her laughter, but I shrugged in my own bit of defiance. She continued to pester me as the banquet continued around us.

After the majority of plates were cleared, the King rose. All noise in the room stopped and we turned to hear what he had to say. "I continue to be concerned with the level of morality here at court." I glanced at Claude, thinking that maybe he would promise to put a stop to the unbridled frivolity that his favorites indulged in on a constant basis. I was sick of constantly monitoring the safety of the demoiselles of the Queen's household. If he were finally listening to his councilors like Louis, I applauded the King.

"As you know, my beloved Mother has tried to set an example of behavior for the ladies and gentlemen at court." At his words, several raised loud toasts to the Queen, who held her own court in the Tuileries. Once the clamor died down, the King resumed his speech, with all eyes upon him. He was clearly enjoying the undivided attention.

"However, I cannot sit idly by while certain members of this court engage in immoral behavior that violates their marital vows." Beside me, Claude snorted; if the King wanted to lecture his courtiers for taking on lovers, he would have a very steep battle to fight. As the crowd leaned forward to see who would be singled out for the King's admonishment, the silence was unnerving. "The Queen and I have worked hard to set an example of marital fidelity for all to follow." At the mention of Queen Louise, I looked at her seat at the King's table. When I did not see her, I began to rise to see if she needed my help.

"I have here letters which make me very sad to see the state of our court as it stands today. And as your God-anointed sovereign, I will not allow such lasciviousness in my court." He pulled out a stack of letters from his doublet, which as always was woven with shining golden thread. Like his sister, Margot, he had a flair for the dramatic and he loved to use it whenever possible. Unfolding the pages, he began to read.

"My dearest," he began, and I noticed that the room sat rapt with attention his every word, "I cannot tell you how much it pains me that you are not with me tonight in Paris." Eyebrows wiggled and several tried to stifle giggles. The gossips of the court were having quite a night.

"When you return from Normandy be assured that I will be there to greet you." At those words, I froze. Those words sounded too familiar. It was possible that there were any number of married women writing men who were away at the Norman campaign. Surely, I was imagining things. The King's next words removed any doubt.

"I spend too many nights virtually alone, lying next to a cold husband," those words were ones that Louis himself wrote, but taken completely out of context and read in front of the court, they were humiliating. My head began to spin and I could only see a white light. I could not face anyone at the banquet, but none of them knew why. No one knew that those words were supposedly written by me.

"Madame de Nevers, you have brought shame to this court." The King looked me straight in the eye as if he was a wolf about to take down his prey. I have never seen a colder look in anyone's eyes and I will never forget it. I have never been at the loss for words, but the shock and humiliation he heaped upon me at that moment were unimaginable.

He held the letters above his head, "Those are your words, are they not?

"Those letters were sent by me, but as you know, Majesty--"

"This is unacceptable. I have given you and your family every honor possible in this court. You live on my largess. Your husband is one of the finest men in France and you," he pointed a long, elegant finger at me. I was still so shocked at the absurdity of his behavior that I could not utter a response, "show no gratitude for either of us."

The entire room pivoted to look at me. I heard an awkward cough, the clatter of silverware as it dropped onto a plate. I had heard of the Valois children viciously tearing at one another, but the experience of seeing it firsthand, of being the victim of such behavior, was horrifying.

A second thought came to me. Had the King inherited the madness of his older brother? Henri III had never had the fits that Charles IX suffered from in the past, but was it possible that his madness surfaced much later in life? Had the King lost touch with his senses? Did France have yet another mad monarch? Whether I had been set up or not, I would choose that as my excuse for the King's erratic behavior that night. In my heart, I knew that it was due to his inherent cruelty.

"Majesty, I believe that I have been falsely accused. I will ask for

your mercy, but if you will excuse me, I think that I should leave."
I curtseyed, determined that if he was indeed mad that I would
show no disrespect to the Crown.

"I believe that you should leave, Madame de Nevers. There is no
place in my court for your kind of loose morality." Taking that as
my leave I fled from the banquet room and hailed my coach. I told
the coachman that he was not to stop until he arrived at the door of
the Hotel de Nevers. The second the door closed, I collapsed into
tears.

"Please tell me that you know what is going on with him."   I
looked at Louis, searching his face for some answer. He only
shook his head slowly. "I wish I knew, Henriette."
I had spent the night before sobbing and when my husband made it
to our home at dawn he immediately came to see me in our
bedchamber. He held me as great tears overtook me and I shook
with the effort. Cooing to me that everything would be all right, he
simply held me until the chambermaid came to bring our breakfast.
"I need to leave Paris. I cannot stand it here."   Before I left, I
would send word to the Queen that I must resign my position as
her Mistress of the Robes effective immediately. I hated to leave
the Queen, but I could not continue to function as a member of the
King's court. Nothing could convince me otherwise. As soon as
possible, I bundled myself and my daughter Marie, barely ten, into
a coach and sped with all haste towards Nevers. Louis and our son
would remain behind in Paris. The ducal palace had suffered from
neglect with Louis and I constantly in Paris and it was as good a
time as ever to see to the upkeep of the house.

"Papa says the King was unkind to you," Marie looked at me with
compassion that tears formed in my eyes.
"He was, dearest. We are never to speak ill of the King, especially
in public, but what he said to me was very cruel."
"So, that is why we are going to the country?" She tried to hide her
excitement at the idea of our trip. I did not blame her for her
excitement, Nevers was a wonderful antidote to the machinations

and cruelty of the court. The last two trips that I had taken to Nevers were cloaked in mourning and as a result, I had no recent happy memories of my time there. I was determined to change that.

"Yes, we are going so that we will not be underfoot of the King and so Papa can get work done without worrying about me. But we will have fun while we are in Nevers, I will make sure of that." At that, my daughter smiled at me. I was looking forward to spending time with her before we made arrangements to send her to her eventual in-laws. The Duc de Mayenne was keen to finalize my daughter's betrothal to his son and heir, and my sister encouraged the match. We would have even stronger ties to the Guise, but no matter how furious I was with the King, I still worried that if we joined in open rebellion against him, we were dooming ourselves. Louis had his own doubts about allying with Mayenne because the week before I left Paris, he openly quarreled with Guise and Mayenne over the King's policy of handling the Duc d'Alceon. Louis started to question the motivations behind both of the brothers. Because of this, I had hesitated in finalizing the betrothal.

We took two days to reach Nevers, starting with the congested road out of Paris. The first evening, we stopped at Gien, where we met the Loire River that would follow us until we reached our home in Nevers. My vassal, the Seigneur of Gien met us at his home, where we stayed the night. At supper, he turned to speak to me. "I am told, My Lady, that the court has grown disgusted with the King's rule."

I nodded, admitting to myself that speaking of the unrest was not speaking against the King, so I could hardly be faulted for doing so. "He listens to few men outside of his dandies and favorites. Even the Queen Mother has lost so much influence that she spends almost all of her time holding a separate court at the Tuileries."

He raised his eyebrow, "The Tuileries stands facing the Louvre; are they now in opposition with one another?" We had long since accepted that the King was his Mother's favorite child and that their bond was unbreakable. Now, even Catherine de Medici found her petted son unmanageable and unreasonable.

"I should warn you, that here in the countryside, men are more given to talk. And many of them question why they should continue to support a King who taxes us into poverty and squanders the money on a few favored dandies."

"I do hope that it is only talk; I do not encourage open rebellion of my vassals and I certainly do not wish to betray the King." If he wished to lure me into a rebellion, I would not fall into that trap. I came to the countryside to escape danger, not to sow seeds of it wherever I went.

"At the moment, yes. There are many loyal Catholics in France who wonder what good loyalty to a King who betrays us will benefit them. As he has no heir other than Alceon, they also worry if the county will immediately fall into heresy once Henri III is no more."

Marie and I continued on to Nevers, looking out towards the Loire as it wound southward. On the second evening, we saw the towers of Nevers and I knew that we were home. As we pulled up to the ducal palace, I felt a swelling of pride. Nowhere else did I feel more the Duchess of Nevers than our family seat. At the top of the stairs leading to the front door, a tower enclosed a spiral staircase, commissioned by my grandfather. The same architect who had designed a more elaborate version at Blois had repeated the exquisite feat for our family home. It was a particular favorite of mine as a child, a place to run and hide while whispering secrets around the winding slabs of stone. A hoyden, I had played with my siblings as we wound down the steps of the staircase, hiding from one another as we did so. I snuck a glance at Marie and I realized that she was thinking of doing the same thing. Only without a brother to play with, she would have to find a companion.

I had no desire to take Charles with us, because the landscape of our home only served to remind me of his precarious position. Directly behind the palace stood the Cathedral de Nevers, where the bodies of his brothers lay. I vowed to spend as little time looking at the cathedral while I was home as I dared. I had no desire to remind myself of the fragility of our lives.

A few days after we settled into the palace, I received several letters from Paris. The first was from my sister Catherine, filled with her indignation at the King's decision to publicly humiliate me. "Now you know what my husband has been forced to endure," she declared. "At least in his case, the King has the decency to do it in private. Only an animal would be crude enough to do that to a lady in public. And in full view of the court! My dear, I cannot imagine how you felt!"

The second letter came from Claude, equally appalled at the King's behavior, but since she had witnessed it firsthand, she was more concerned with how I was dealing with the public humiliation. "I have heard that you resigned as Mistress of The Robes and I completely agree with you. No one should have to see that insufferable man every day, given how vilely he treated you."

The third came from Louis, who opened with asking how I was faring and asking after Marie. The King, he wrote, made no reference to his treatment of me, acting as if it never happened. So far, he had said nothing to Louis about my resignation and withdrawal from court. The rest of the letter caused me great concern. The Plague had come to Paris, spread this time from Spain. After taking the Queen of Spain's life, it quickly swept into Paris the Summer of 1581 and Louis began to fear for Charles' life. I was just as fearful that our son was in danger. Quickly pulling out pen and paper, I wrote a quick letter to Louis that I as much as it pained me to separate him from our children, perhaps he should send Charles to Nevers to stay with me. Calling for a page, I sent the letter to Paris posthaste.

"Madame, you have a visitor." My chambermaid appeared at the doorway and bobbed a quick curtsey.

"Who is it?" I had no plans to see anyone that day. If anything, Marie and I were to spend a quiet day walking in the palace gardens. I was relishing the opportunity to play mother to my remaining daughter without the demands of the court pulling at my sleeve.

"The Bishop of Nevers." I frowned; like most Bishops, he rarely spent time to tend his own flock in person and tarried in Paris to solidify his personal interests. I could not fathom why he was in Nevers.

"Madame la Duchess!" He swept into the room and gave me a quick kiss on the cheek. Settling into a chair next to me, he began to speak.

"Forgive me for intruding, but I was just informed that you are here. I heard of the King's behavior in Paris." I groaned inwardly —if word had traveled to Nevers so quickly, it had spread everywhere. Perhaps, I would do well to remain unseen for a while.

"That behavior is beneath a Christian King and I am appalled by it. I am especially appalled that it happened to my own liege lady. If I may say, this does not sound like the woman I have known since she was a babe."

"May I confess something to you?" At that, he nodded. "The King himself asked me to write those letters, claiming that he wanted to catch his Mignon in an attempted seduction of the Queen. I agreed to do so and Louis worked hand in hand with me in writing those letters. As a matter of fact, Louis wrote most of them."

"That romantic fool! Forgive me, this is no laughing matter." He leaned forward as if to convey to me his deepest secrets. "I have been a staunch supporter of the King. When he took the throne, he made a spectacle of himself, flagellating in the street and attending services. I was under the impression that he was a Godly man."

I raised my eyebrows, "And now?'

He excelled a long sigh. "I have read several reports that the King engages in sexual relations with these male favorites. In this, he is flaunting God's teachings. As a man of the cloth, I cannot support a man who flagrantly flouts the Church's laws."

I nodded again, "I understand." Still, I did not want to encourage rebellion or to be seen caught up in inciting one.

"Yet, I wish that this behavior was the only thing that worries me about this King. He has shown his contempt for the noble families of France by promoting these base men. The taxes he has raised are ruining our treasury. Madame," he looked directly at me, "I fear that this King may bring about the ruin of France."

"Do you think that he is as mad as his brother was?" I had not broached the subject with anyone other than Louis. The Bishop simply shrugged in response.

"I do not know if I am fit to judge the soundness of any man's mind, but I do believe that this prince is not fit to rule. Despite his mother's desire to put him on a throne, I do not think that he is fit to sit on any Earthly throne."

"Bishop, I understand your fear, but as the wife of one of the King's most important counselors, I have no plans to put myself in open rebellion against him. Louis and I could not afford my doing such a foolish thing."

"My Lady, there are many people who would tell you that the man who sits on the throne and the kingdom are one and the same. However, this King has shown that in his misrule, he will do all that he can do to destroy that kingdom. I believe that our loyalty is first to France and secondly to the man who sits on Her throne."

"But, did not God, Himself, put the man on the throne?" Louis and I both believed in the principle that God chose our sovereign and that to rebel against our king, we were also rebelling against God, Himself. Despite our growing disenchantment with this particular king, our belief in his right to rule was unshakable.

"Perhaps Satan, himself, has poisoned his mind and now it is the duty of Christians to help him to leave it." Those words scared me; was I looking at the beginnings of a true rebellion against the king?

A week later, a coach appeared at the courtyard of the palace, bearing two occupants, my sleepy son and his nurse. "The Duc is terrified that the Plague will continue to ravage Paris and he told me that I was to come to you as soon as possible."

I pulled Charles into my arms and he gave a sleepy whine. "I'll send word to the Duc immediately to tell him that you've arrived safely."

She curtsied and I noticed that she looked uncomfortable. "What is it?"

She wrung her hands, "People in Paris are saying that the Plague is

God's punishment for the King's sinful relationships with his favorites."

So, word of the King's unnatural activities had made it to the masses and the superstitious amongst them were already blaming things on him. Previously, I had thought that the threat was limited to a few disgruntled nobles. Perhaps the anger was more widespread than I had assumed.

"What else are they saying?" I led the girl into the house and towards the nursery.

"That they need a man who will stand for Paris. They are looking for a champion. Many of them are asking that the Duc de Guise stand up for them."

"I will do nothing that will jeopardize Louis' position at court; I want to make that perfectly clear." I glanced at the women assembled in my salon that January morning of 1583. To my left sat my sister Catherine, determined as always to play an active role in opposing the King. Her mother-in-law, Anna, the Duchess of Nemours, formerly the Dowager Duchess de Guise, sat beside her. On the other side of Catherine sat the Duchess of Montpensier, Anna's only daughter and the biggest firebrand of criticism against the King's rule. For moral support, Claude sat at my own right, ready to give her advice and hopefully balance the extremism of Montpensier.

"Henriette, you are practically one of us," Montpensier leaned forward to take a cake from the table in front of us. "Other than my brother, few have suffered under the King as much as you have."

"And I plan to suffer as little as possible in the future." I turned to Anna, who like Louis, was an Italian and one of the closest friends of the Queen Mother. "Are you sure that Catherine can do nothing more to reason with her son?" I mourned the old days when the court quaked at the sight of Catherine de Medici's shadow crossing a threshold. To think that it was her pampered favorite son who neutered her power, was galling to all of us.

Anna shook her head, "We have both done everything that we can to address the King in a maternal fashion, he is well beyond reason." She shot a harsh look at Montpensier, who was about to interrupt her mother. Montpensier wisely shut up as soon as her mother looked at her.

"I have to raise this issue and I'm sure you're all in particular tired of hearing it. I will be seen as fully putting in my fortunes with the 'Guise faction.' I mean no disrespect to any of you, but you do know that any criticism you all face for being power-hungry will also fall on me. I had planned on taking a neutral stance." I glanced at Anna, who by right, led the female portion of the 'Guise faction.' To her credit, she did not look offended.

"France needs a strong leader and ultimately, we all serve France, not a man." She echoed what the Bishop had told me in Nevers, which still made me uncomfortable. That the Malcontents and the adherents of the growing Catholic League parroted a single line made me wonder if they were less patriots and more fanatics. I started to worry about Marie, who had left for Joinville to get to know her own betrothed, Mayenne's heir and Anna's grandson. The granddaughter of King Louis XII, Anna was conscious of her royal heritage. It was her tie to the older Capets, who ruled France for centuries, combined with her genuine friendship with the Queen Mother that made her such a valuable ally at court.

"Tell me, if Henri were to lose the throne, who would take his place? My cousin Navarre?" At the mention of Navarre, Montpensier winced. This time, Anna could not stop her from speaking.

"France is a Catholic nation and it will continue to be so. As a heretic, Navarre is barred from inheriting the throne. As we all know, His Holiness will soon bar him from the succession." I lifted my eyebrow at that. While all Catholics owed the Pope loyalty, kings and nations were not very keen on the Pope making pronouncements on the succession of their monarchs. In my opinion, the Pope was reaching too far, but I kept that opinion to myself. Besides, Navarre had changed religion once and nothing stopped him from doing so again in order to take the throne.

"Henriette, we only want you to open your home to members of the court, just like the salons that you held at Claude's home."

Claude groaned at the mention of her home; the building was a virtual dust pile while renovations to store up rotting wood stretched on. Catherine had volunteered my home as a replacement, which was why the group were assembled in my salon that cold morning.

"I will not allow political speeches, or talk of rebellion against the King. This is Louis' home and I will not endanger him by doing something stupid." I looked directly at Montpensier, who gave a flippant shrug.

"Very well—you can simply provide entertainment, while the political discussions continue at my home. The orators are more than welcome there, anyway."

"Do you think that Margot will attend?" Catherine would love to have the King's sister give her blessings to our activities through her presence. I, however, remembered the terror in Margot's eyes years earlier, when she realized the King would blame her for Alceon's rebellion. Margot's position was even weaker since Alceon began exhibiting the signs of tuberculosis the previous June, the second of Catherine de Medici's sons to suffer from the illness. Without Alceon, Margot would be bereft of influential allies at court and I had no desire to place her in any sort of jeopardy either. "If Margot feels comfortable, she will come. Knowing that we won't be witness to seditious talk at my home will make it easier for her to attend."

"Well, then, it's settled. You will provide the lighthearted entertainment for the court, while I provide a haven for its deserters." Montpensier popped another cake into her mouth.

"That reminds me, I want to make sure we do nothing to usurp the Queen's position as first lady of the court." I would never forget her kindness to me when Francis died suddenly and she had earned my lifelong amity for what she had done for me.

"Henriette, Louise has no desire to be a social leader," Anna interjected. "Given how that horrible woman," she set her jaw at the mention of the Queen's step-mother, "shut her up like a house maid, it's no wonder Louise wants to withdraw to the quiet of her chambers."

I looked at Anna. "Then, it's settled, no humiliation of the Queen."

"You were adamant that these were not to be political gatherings, right?" Louis glanced at our salon, which was packed with people.
"Yes, I looked Montpensier right in the eye and demanded it. If this gathering turns political, you are to escort them out into the street."
"Let's hope it doesn't."   He glanced over to a corner where the Spanish ambassador, Mendoza, chatted with nobles known to be sympathetic to the gathering Catholic League. I groaned inwardly, hoping that rumors would not reach the King's ears that I was supplying money to Phillip of Spain and his Catholic League. Phillip was eager to pick up support from any disgruntled Catholics, no matter where they lived in Europe. Just to be safe, I would spend Mass the next morning on my knees, praying for protection for myself and the rest of my family.
I felt another strong gust of wind and looked to my side to see my brother-in-law, the Duc de Guise stride into the packed salon.   .
"Do you always walk accompanied by so much wind, brother?" At my teasing, he laughed. "It's the outcome of being so tall. I control the elements, I'm afraid. This is a wonderful gathering," he added.
"Just be sure that it is not filled with political dealings. I still want to keep this neutral ground."
He nodded, "I do enough meetings at the Hotel de Guise and at my sister's house. You have my word on it." Despite his reputation, I began to earnestly like my hot-headed brother-in-law. He always kept his word to me. While he and Catherine were always having a row, he treated me with the upmost respect. As he walked away, I turned to listen to the poet I had hired for the evening. I stuck with love as the theme, thinking that it was one of the safest.
Holding court in the midst of the audience, Margot sat, her hair adorned with a long ostrich feather. Fed up with her husband's philandering, she had returned to the French court to try her luck as an exiled Queen. So far, my friend found my home a safe haven from her brother's boisterous court. At Margot's hand, a handsome

man whispered to her. From the look on his face, he found her utterly irresistible. "Oh, no, Margot. Not again," I shook my head, but I knew that it was pointless to try to dissuade her from a new love affair. With enough money from her dowry and loans from friends like Claude, Margot set up her own household in a hotel near the Louvre, which meant that she enjoyed more freedom than she had seen before in France or in Navarre.

Margot has suffered the same humiliation that I did. On a hot August night, she made her way to the Louvre, to preside over a banquet as was her due with Louise and the Queen Mother absent. As the King had done with me, he spent the entire evening luring his sister into a false sense of security. Near the end of the evening, he railed against her, accusing her of conceiving her latest lover's child. He had the audacity to claim that her "excesses" were ruining his Mignon's "morals." As if those criminals ever had any morals! Never one to give up without a fight, Margot employed her considerable letter-writing skills to defend herself. The King responded by banishing her from France.

To her credit, as soon as the Queen Mother heard of this charade, she went to her son and demanded that he work to reconcile himself with his sister. Navarre also came to Margot's defense, unwilling to allow his own Queen to endure the humiliation of a fellow sovereign. Navarre's pride had been wounded, but he had no desire to admit his queen back into his own kingdom. Margot sat in limbo, unable to leave France but unable to enter Navarre. A lesser woman would have bemoaned her situation; Margot used it as an excuse for revelry.

The Queen Mother finally employed her skills at reconciliation and took an active hand in their King's behavior. Now the King had gone too far, humiliating his remaining sibling and alienating an ally against Spain. Catherine de Medici, more than anyone, recognized how vulnerable the King's position was. Cracks were openly forming between the King and his Catholic supporters, which led them to add their support to the Catholic League openly. Now Catholics had a legitimate alternative to remaining loyal to the crown.

Plague returned to Paris that summer and to escape the illness, the King moved the court to St. Germain. Louis and I were unwilling to take any chances, so Charles and I joined him at St. Germain. I hooted with laughter when Louis told me that the King sent men across France to hear of their concerns. "If he really cared, he would have asked in 1574."

At St. Germain, the Cardinal Bourbon and Duc de Guise began a friendship, one motivated by Bourbon's belief that he should be the next Dauphin. "My husband has another candidate," Catherine confessed to me one day as we walked amongst the Italian gardens of St. Germain. There was not a soul within earshot, so we could talk freely.

"Who?"

"The eldest son of the Duc de Lorraine. As Princess Claude's son, he is Henry II's grandson. The Queen Mother cannot say no to her own grandson."

"But, will she say no to a cousin of the Guise?"

She shrugged, "Henri plans to make her see that the boy is the only candidate."

"So, the League plots against itself?"

"No, my husband believes that the League can ally itself with the King and avoid open conflict with him if he accepts his own nephew as his heir. It would avoid bloodshed. That is what you and Louis want, isn't it?'

"Catherine, do you really think that given the League's rhetoric, that it exists only for the purpose of putting a boy on the throne? I doubt it; it goes much further than that."

She put up her hands, "Sure, there are some that want open warfare, some that want to rid the world of Navarre and others who would be happier if Phillip of Spain were King of France. There are so many who have united against the King that they have different ways of getting rid of the King."

"It's this disorder and squabbling that makes me hesitate in supporting it. That and the danger of being thrown into the dungeons for treason."

"I am leaving for Rome," Louis slid that bit of information to me while we were preparing for bed as August turned into September. "Are you on a mission from the King?'

He nodded, "Officially, it is all that my trip is for. I have another reason for seeing the Holy See. I want to ask the Pope to weigh in on whether this Catholic League is legal."

"You mean, you want to know if their plans to usurp Navarre are legitimate?"

"That, too. I also want to know if the Pope would actually support Frenchmen who support the Spanish king in opposing the King."

"What will you do if the Pope gives the League his blessing?"

"Officially, I will still support the King, but my true alliance will be with the League. I can't remain neutral for much longer. Guise confides in me constantly and I've begun to see the wisdom in his reasoning."

"Catherine does the same to me, but I admit I've got my reservations."

He nodded and gave me a small smile. "There is another reason why I want to go to Rome. My brother has no heirs and I want to ask the Pope for his support in naming me Duc de Mantua."

"Do you think there's a chance of him doing so?" Louis was a male heir, but given the fact that this title was Italian and not French, a different law applied. We did not have substantial Italian holdings since Louis was the designated heir of his family's French holdings, so we had little experience in dealing with the inheritance laws of Lombardy. There was no more powerful ally in Italy than the Pope, however.

"What should I do while you're away in Rome? Should I cancel the salons?"

He shook his head, "Continue our policy of neutrality. It's been the best one for us so far and I think that it's wisest if we continue with it."

A week later, four-year-old Charles and I stood at the courtyard of St. Germain, where the court stayed to avoid the plague sweeping across Paris,, and we bid adieu to my husband. Our family was down to two people. I hoped that he would return soon and with news that would decide our own position on the succession of France.

Louis' trip to Rome meant that we spent more than half that year apart, united only by our letters. Papal politics were an art onto themselves, one that few were brave or patient enough to enter. When Louis had mentioned that he wished to go to Rome, I assumed that he felt he had a strong claim to his older brother's Duchy. As the months passed on, however, Louis and I learned firsthand just how slowly things progressed at the Holy See.

Louis' letters told of his ongoing frustration. *"I have approached the Pope several times about Mantua; he somehow manages to talk for hours, yet say nothing. I thought that the King was difficult, yet the Pope is more exasperating."* He hoped to get more encouraging news about the legitimacy of the League, but without solid victories, the Pope held on endorsing it until it was politically expedient to do so. Other than lavishing my attention on my son, letters were all that I had of my family. Catherine wrote to tell me of her deepening friendship with her betrothed. As I had hoped, the Orleans were an excellent match for my eldest daughter and they did nothing to try and damper her spirit. I had worried that Marie de Bourbon, our kinswoman, could be a liability as years before the King imprisoned her for harboring Protestants. Given how nebulous the future of France's leadership and religion were, I soon realized that a family friendly to Protestantism would be a good thing for my daughter. I sternly cautioned her not to attend Protestant services, however. There was plenty of time in the future for her to question her faith as my sister Marie did.

My daughter Marie wrote me from Joinville, where the entire Guise clan had descended to mourn the loss of the first Duchess de Guise. Antoinette de Bourbon, another of our distant relations, had finally succumbed to old age and the Guise were bereft without their matriarch. Catherine spent her childhood at the Dowager Duchess's knee and saw her husband's grandmother as her own family. The loss of her surrogate grandmother hit her hard.

Generations of French girls grew up in Joinville where they learned the skills of becoming noble wives, while the Duchess worked to secure matches for each girl under her care. As a result, many noble women in France owed their loyalty to the Guise from an early age and that loyalty was embodied in the Dower Duchess de Guise.

I continued to keep a watchful eye on Mayenne and his sister, hoping that neither of them did anything to cause me to regret my younger daughter's betrothal. So far, none of the Guise had done anything to cause me alarm. If anything, we were growing closer to the Guise cause by necessity, while the King continued to alienate even his most ardent allies.

While Louis publicly declared his loyalty to the King for all to hear, in private, we both maintained close ties with Guise. We were firmly in agreement with the League, but could not afford to offend the King. Marie continued to flourish at Joinville and we set her wedding date for a few months after her eighteenth birthday. In Paris, I remained close with the band of Guise women and when asked, I simply responded that the King's treatment of me drove me to find friendship with those who were most injured by him. In those days, I scarcely think that the King cared that I did not support him. He probably thought of me not at all.

I continued to enjoy the camaraderie of the Guise women and the freedom of responsibility of managing the Queen's household. My current position was perfect for me, with all of the respect that came from my family and my marriage without any obligations at court. I was free to come and go as I pleased. While Louis played the politician in Rome, I straddled the two camps of Catholic retainers and enjoyed my stated neutrality.

Being a silent part of the opposition to the King meant that I could still afford to watch the activities of the League as an insider and as a detached observer. Realizing that he could not make a claim for the crown openly, Guise continued to put forth our kinsman, the Cardinal de Bourbon, as the heir to Henri III. Unlike me, my sister Catherine had no reservations about speaking her mind openly, as she often did while sitting beside me at Montpensier's salons.

"He dotes on the Cardinal. My husband stands next to him, hat doffed and in his hand, and refers to him as 'Monsieur.'" As soon as Bourbon leaves, he calls him 'the Little Man.'"

"Does Bourbon even know that he's laughing at him behind his back?"

"No, it's become an open joke amongst us. Oh, that reminds me," she snorted before she could stop herself, "Henry actually suggested to the Cardinal that he marry Catherine of Navarre. And he is actually considering it! What an imbecile!" She fanned herself, more so from the exertion than shame.

"Wouldn't they need a dispensation?" Catherine was his own niece. The practicalities of such a marriage made me dizzy.

"Probably, but no one seriously plans on going through with the plan. Bourbon is the only one stupid enough to think that they're serious." Truth be told, no one in our family could stand my Uncle. In addition to being incredibly gullible, he was also selfish and incredibly vain. According to my nurse, I hated him the first time I saw him, choosing to bite him rather than greet him. Unfortunately, as my mother's only remaining brother, he was the next in line to the throne.

"Catherine, if he takes the throne, he'll need an heir."

"If he has no one, then the crown will fall to..." she rolled her eyes in a mock-innocent gesture.

"Surely you don't think that the country will accept your son as the Dauphin." Perhaps the Leaguers' ideas were more absurd than I'd feared. If they expected the young Prince de Joinville to become the next Dauphin, they were stretching too far.

Catherine dropped her fan in her lap. "Henriette, someone has to be King! My son is a Bourbon and as a Guise he is a Capet. His pedigree is impeccable and France needs a King of royal French blood. Surely you don't want to give Spain a pretext for taking the throne of France!"

"With all of the money Phillip is pouring into the League, doesn't he own it already? Your husband should be careful to whom he owes money. Phillip will ask for his due sooner or later."

"Phillip has been asking for many things recently."

"Oh, how is that?" I knew better than to take the bait when Catherine had my curiosity roused, but I always fell for that trap.

"He's been corresponding with Margot recently. She's thinking of divorcing Navarre and becoming Phillip's next Queen."

I had not heard of this, even when Margot and I were alone together. "You have to be mistaken about that. Why would Margot agree to marry her sister's husband?"

Catherine shrugged, "She is married to a heretic. Phillip would likely ally with the King, at least in public, if he were once again married to his sister. It might elevate Margot in her brother's eyes."

I could not fault Margot for trying to outsmart the King; his cruelty towards her was the only thing worse than his cruelty towards me. After Phillip's fourth wife had died of the plague five years earlier, he had yet to find a fifth. Still, the idea of marrying his dead wife's sister sounded repugnant.

"Where do you hear such things, Catherine?" If she was conspiring, I would have to try to reason with her. I had no desire for my sister to implicate herself in a conspiracy and languish in prison at the King's pleasure.

"Not at court. Since the Queen Mother gave up hope of influencing her son, she spends most of her time writing letters at the Tuileries. This information came directly from my husband's spies."

The Queen Mother's palace sat directly across from the Louvre, yet the distance between her and her favorite child might have been an ocean's width. The Mignons, led by the Duc d'Epernon, whispered in the King's ear that his Mother had also turned against him. Faced with few allies at the heart of power, Catherine de Medici had turned to making an alliance with the Guise. My sister's star was in ascendancy just as her husband's was and she knew it.

The Summer of 1584, the fortunes of the entire Valois family changed for the worse. The Duc d'Alceon, the King's younger brother and heir, died of tuberculosis. Before his death, Catholics across France held out hope that our childless King would be succeeded by a Catholic monarch. Henry of Navarre was previously just a worst-case scenario, a kind of contingency plan if all of the Valois princes died without an heir.

The League went into action, working to do anything to keep a Protestant from ascending to the throne of France. As Catholics, our worst nightmare would soon come true and with the King's death, we would descend into heresy.

Eventually, even the King began to notice that his support outside of his sycophantic Mignons was dwindling. In September, a letter arrived from the Louvre, bearing the King's own seal. As my page handed it to me, I could not stop a groan from escaping my throat. I placed it on my desk and resolved to dally as long as I could before opening it. I managed to fill my day with empty activities until almost supper. Eventually a macabre sense of curiosity overtook me. I opened the letter to see what the King had to say.

"Ma Cousine," he must want something since he resorted to addressing me as "Cousine" once again. *"Having found an opportunity to write to you, you have me hopelessly in your hands; not, however, to trouble your repose, but to assure you that the affection I bore you before you quitted the Court has not diminished;"* I snorted at this. His definition of "affection" was clearly not the same as mine. *"on the contrary, it has gathered strength; so that as long as I live, I vow to bear you all honor and love, and to demean myself as your very faithful relative and good friend."*

Oh, God help me, the man wanted my "friendship?" What kind of trickery was he about? The languid joy I had felt for the past four years melted away. Despite the flowery words, he wanted something from me. The question was just how much he wanted from me. The letter continued with more flattery, enough to make me feel nauseated. I scanned the rest of the letter, looking for the favor that I knew he would eventually ask of me.

"Adieu, ma bonne cousine, I am yours entirely; and say the same to M. de Nevers, as you will both soon experience. Return hither soon; for it is not seemly that you should both be absent from the court for so long a period. I kiss your hand, ma cousine, a

thousand times. HENRY." Ah, there was my answer. The King was terrified that Louis would desert him. I had no idea if he had spies telling him that Louis was considering joining the League. I knew for a fact that Louis wanted to continue playing a middle way as long as possible, although hopefully the King did not know that. Flattering me was his best hope for also flattering Louis.

About a week later, Louis returned from Italy. He strode into our bedchamber, covered in dirt from the road, but I cared little for how he looked or smelled. I simply wanted my husband in my arms. For just a moment, I wanted to forget the court and have him all to myself.

"The King has been busy writing me." At that, Louis' eyebrows shot up.

"What did he say?"

"He gave me vague promises that he admires me and begged me to intervene with you on his behalf. He must be getting desperate."

Louis expelled a deep sigh. "He is. He's sounding out the loyalty of everyone, including me. I've assured him several times that I will back him, but he's like Charles when he thinks that we aren't paying attention to him. He needs assurance from everyone around him."

"And being King, he will neither apologize nor take responsibility for alienating his nobles." I rolled my eyes.

"Exactly. He's offered me a governorship as soon as one becomes available."

"Available! They're not 'available' because he's already given them to his friends!" I shook my head, marveling at the King's arrogance.

"He's done worse, much worse. Or at least, his friends urged him to do so. He's allowed them to pen an edict stating that the King of France is not subject to any acts by the Pope that he disagrees with. And," he looked at me, "that includes a Papal bull, interdict or even excommunication."

My mouth fell open. If the King were to issue such an edict, it would mean that he placed himself above the Holy Father. "But that would mean that he would basically be--"

"A Protestant."

"Will he be stupid enough to go through with such an act?"

Louis shook his head, "I don't know—but if it were to be issued, it would pave the way for Navarre to rule. Perhaps in some way, the King would be making his rule official."

"But he would lose the support of virtually every faithful Catholic in the kingdom."

"Starting with Guise."

The Guise were well aware that the idea of such an edict was possible; in fact, they used it as propaganda against the King as soon as word leaked out of St. Germain that there was the merest whisper of it happening. No Catholic cleric in France would dare address the edict in the pulpit and emboldened with this latest development, the Cardinal de Bourbon began loudly declaring his support for the League. Catholics were splintering faster than the kingdom at large and only the King was unable to see it.

"Any commitment from the Pope? Or any progress on Mantua?"

Louis shook his head and I began to see how tired he was from his journey.

"Now, they see me as a foreigner. I followed Catherine to the French court and I accepted my grandmother's French lands. Those two acts alone have branded me a Frenchman. Now, no man in Lombardy wants to accept me as Duke." He exhaled a long sigh.

A selfish part of me felt relieved that we would not be taking over the lands of Mantua. I understood Louis' desire to take over what should have been his birthright. After all, I had taken over my lands for my brother James after his death. Louis should have been allowed to do the same thing. Yet administering foreign domains was not easy, as I had learned when Louis made the decision to sell my lands in Flanders without my consent. Lands out of sight were all too easily given to another.

Unlike my husband, I considered myself thoroughly French and had no desire to reign as Duchess in Italy. France might be splintering under a foolish monarch, but I was determined to stay and fight for her.

A few days later, Louis departed for St. Germain in an attempt to reason with the King and counter the nonsense his favorites were whispering in his ear. If nothing else, surely Louis could convince the King to avoid insulting and alienating the Vatican. Without the Pope's help, faced with Phillip II's deep pockets and surrounding Protestant nations, the King was politically isolated.

"I scarcely know which way to place my own allegiance," he confessed to me at the end of another long day. "The Cardinals Guise and Bourbon keep interrupting the meetings, arguing over points of theology one minute and precedence the next." My uncle, the Cardinal of Bourbon was growing more and more stupid in his behavior. The Cardinal de Guise, younger brother of the Duc de Guise, was a powerful member of the same League that put forth Bourbon as the strongest Catholic candidate for the heir to the throne. Alienate the Cardinal de Guise and Bourbon would lose his allies, but only my uncle would be foolish enough to not realize the danger he caused.

"Another 'vital' issue to the kingdom, was the issue over how extravagantly the women should dress. "He still occupies himself with issues of etiquette in lieu of actual decision and policy making. The Queen herself caught Madame de Neuill, wife of the President of the Parliament of Paris buying fabrics reserved only for the nobility. The outcry took days to resolve. This is what our government is distracted with! Sometimes, I think that I would get more done sitting on the floor, playing with Charles."

"Now more than ever, I know that it was wise to strike a middle road between the King's supporters and those of the League's. Neither of them seem capable of putting together a viable plan for the future of the country. France is becoming more and more vulnerable to invasion."

At least the absence of the Ducs de Joyeuse and d'Epernon meant that the King was available to meet with Louis on a regular basis. *"The King confessed the d'Epernon was in Pau to lure Navarre back to Catholicism. If he could do so, then the League's power would be minimized and I would have no reason to ally with Guise. I pray more than most that d'Epernon will succeed. Joyeuse*

*is at home, convalescing, so we are spared his presence for the
moment. Once they return, however, the King has decreed that
each shall be treated as Princes of the Blood. All rules of
deportment are suspended for them and they are to approach his
apartments at any hour."*

The King had elevated his favorites to the level of his own
brothers, treating them better than he had ever treated his own
siblings. Previously, the complaints of the nobles against the King
made them look like children squabbling over precedence. With
this elevation, it was becoming apparent that the King was
determined to undermine the structure of the nobility of France.

The members of the Catholic League began to draw lines against
the King, first by recruiting loyal clients in the Northern and
Eastern reaches of the kingdom. Fearing that the Spanish would
attack France from the West, the King began looking for foreign
sources to lend money to the royal treasury. The moment the
King's royal envoy entered Lorraine on his way to beg for money
in Switzerland, however, the Duc de Lorraine stated his
determination to openly rebel against the King. The envoy was
promptly arrested and detained, pending payment from the King.

None of the talk of politics mattered to me as Charles was struck
down with a fever. It has spread throughout his body, at first
causing him to scream with pain. As the days dragged on, however,
exhaustion sapped his strength and he rarely slept without
becoming fretful. *Dear God, he is only five-years-old—will God
take him away from me,* I wondered? Were I a more pious woman,
I would race to the chapel in the Hotel de Nevers and plead to God
for his life. Luckily, word immediately came to my sister Catherine
and the Queen Mother in St. Germain, and the two spent hours on
their knees praying for my son's life. I cared not one whit for
politics; Guise and Valois prayers were the same when my son's
life was at stake.

They were not the only ones who pleaded with the Almighty to
spare my remaining son. The Guise women, the Duchess de
Nemours and Montpensier also sent prayers to Heaven to save

Charles. With their fingers on their rosaries, their efforts freed me to spend my hours at Charles' bedside, wiping his feverish body down and singing to him to calm him.

I had a cot brought into Charles' room so that I could attend him constantly and be at his side whenever he needed me. "Madame, I am not sure, but I think that it could be contagious," the physician Mouzon warned me. With no faith left in the men who could not save my two older sons, I had sent for a new man to tend to him and Monsieur Mouzon came highly recommended by the Duchess de Nemours.

"If God sees fit to take me, then he may have me. My husband can raise our son and I have no desire to continue living with a third son buried in our crypt at the cathedral in Nevers." I snapped at him, not caring for manners at the moment. I am sure he had seen his fill of worried mothers hovering over a sick child, and he only placed his hands on my shoulder and left the room without uttering another word.

I spent the month of November tending to my son, willing him to eat and drink, and hoping that all the effort would convince God to allow this son to live. I scarcely noticed when the Advent season brought on the chill of December to Paris. The King allowed Louis to leave St. Germain for the season and to help me in tending to Charles in Paris. While I read each of Louis' letters, in my state, it was difficult to remember when Louis would return. I was too ensconced in my ever-shrinking world of anguish.

On the fourth of December, the door to Charles' room quietly opened. Thinking it was the physician or a maid, I did not turn to see who stood behind me. Louis' large hand cupped around mine and I realized that my husband was finally home. Turning to him, I allowed him to hold me while I wept.

"The Queen asked me to give this to you." He placed a small rosary into my hands. As tears slid down my cheek, I fingered the small beads, hoping that they would keep me from fully giving in to my emotions. They failed to keep me from doing so and I began to wail like a wounded animal.

"Don't fret so, Henriette. The physician told me that he is through the worst of it. The fever has broken."

I shook my head. Two tiny coffins told me otherwise. I could not relax until my son was on his feet and up to his old antics once again.

"You dare to argue with me? Your own husband?" He was teasing me and the idea that he would do so in the midst of my worry caused me to snort despite myself.

"Louis, you are inappropriate." I glared at him, but he was determined to break my mournful mood.

"Look, he's sleeping. Walk with me for just a few moments, please?" It was a small request and I did need a break from my seated position. I nodded and allowed him to pull me from the room. He held my hand as we walked along the corridor to our own bedchamber.

"Joyeuse has allied himself with the Duc de Lorraine." At his statement, my mouth dropped open. Together with the Duc d'Epernon, the two men virtually ruled the King and France. The King allowed them to style themselves above the rest of the court, which was at the heart of the grudges the Guise and Lorraine relations bore against the King. Joyeuse was married to Queen Louise's sister. There were no other men in the kingdom who owed more to the King's largesse. If one of the Mignons had deserted the King, what did that mean?

"Does that mean the King will desert his favorites? What about the Guise?"

"d'Epernon continues to cozy up to the King. In his case," Louis rolled his eyes in disgust, "there really is no change. The King continues to listen to his counsel as much as he listens to mine, sometimes more. But the King does realize that he will have to keep his loyal advisors close to him. It's why he told me to come home for Christmas and I hate to tell you this at such a time, but he drew up papers for Catherine to inherit the Duchy of Nevers at my death."

I nodded, thankful that Louis had been looking out for our children's inheritance. If, God forbid, we lost Charles, we would not lose everything and our eldest daughter would become the next

Duchess de Nevers.

"I probably don't have to tell you that this largess comes at the cost of my continued loyalty to the King and his cause." Of course it did; nothing from Henri Valois came for free.

"What will you do, Louis? Where do you stand?" Now that I had him in front of me, I could ask him about his plans directly. We could debate our options in real time without the waiting for the post to send his responses.

He looked down at his hands, "I haven't really decided. Guise has asked to meet with me tomorrow morning. He's been at his headquarters in Chalons-sur-Marne."

"Headquarters?" My head snapped up. My isolation from the politics dividing France meant that I was woefully uninformed about the maneuverings around me. If Guise had men that close to Paris, he was less than a day's march to the city. "Did he tell you what the men are for?"

Louis nodded, "Officially, they are at the King's disposal until the money from England comes to hire more Swiss mercenaries. The king is frantically trying to raise the money to get his envoy out of France, which will cut deeply into royal funds. Once he has Swiss money, the King is determined to use Guise's troops to pursue a siege on the city of Antwerp.

His face darkened. "Unofficially, they are there to ensure that the King behaves himself." We both knew that there was little hope that the King would do so.

The next morning before breakfast, my hulking brother-in-law strode into the front salon of the Hotel de Nevers. "Sister," he enveloped me in a warm hug. Guise was born with the personal touch that drew the common people to his standard, bolstering his popularity while alienating the people from the King. The common people had made their choice and Guise was the leader they wanted to lead France. Once Guise chose to use that charisma against the King, the people would immediately follow. At the moment, however, he was simply offering his support for Charles.

"How is the boy?" He looked into my eyes, the eyes that had lost a child before and felt compassion for my situation.

"He is better. The physician thinks that if he continues to improve the next week or so, he may well survive this."

Guise nodded. "I think that if he does so, Henriette, you should both go to Nevers."

His statement grabbed my attention. Guise had never held a secret from me, his respect for me, even when we argued over money years before. He respected me too much to try to deceive me. His respect was due to my position as his sister-in-law and one of the most influential women in France. I had always appreciated that fact, and I pressed the issue further.

"Henri, I know that you are here to talk to my husband and forgive me for being a little behind in the maneuvering in the coming war against Spain, but I would like to know your mind at the moment. Are you here to fight against the Spanish or against the King?"

He pursed his lips. "I only want to save France from heresy. It's touched my family too much for me to sit by and allow it to destroy the country. My wife was married to a heretic. My grandmother almost gave her life in the misguided belief that the heresy was legitimate. Your sister was married to one of the worst heretics in France, one who almost overthrew the King before he could even sit on his throne." He glanced at me, worried that in mentioning my cousin the Prince de Conde he had gone too far. I shook my head, determined to reassure him.

"No, I have more reason to hate Conde than you do. As a matter of fact, I'm grateful to you and your late grandmother for taking my niece in and keeping her safe from her father. How is she?"

He smiled, the wrinkles in the corners of his eyes deepening. "Just as magnetic as her mother was," he crossed himself in the memory of Marie. Catherine de Conde was almost ten and almost of an age to marry. I had made the right decision in placing her in the safekeeping of the Duchess de Guise.

"Catherine and I will have to arrange her marriage soon. I trust you have a candidate in mind?" I lifted my eyebrows and he nodded his head.

Guise scratched his chin, "I think that she would be a good wife to the son of Lorraine. Catherine de Medici may not have had Marie for a daughter-in-law, but she might have Marie's daughter for her grandson."

I looked at Louis; the King had no heirs and the eldest son of the Duc de Lorraine would be the strongest candidate for the throne. As the son of the king's elder sister, Claude, the boy was an attractive candidate. "Wouldn't you want a more illustrious candidate for Lorraine?"

"Actually," he crossed his legs at the ankles, "I would want a girl who has grown up at Joinville and who understands the needs of the houses of Lorraine and Guise." He raised his eyebrows at me, his charm becoming infectious. I realized why Catherine often forgave her husband and why she had given him so many children over their marriage.

"But aren't your placing your alliance with the King of Spain in jeopardy?" It was an open secret that Guise took Spanish money to lead the League. Following the King in going to war against Spain was one thing; it was simply following royal policy. Taking an extremely eligible prince away from a Spanish princess might well be going too far in the powerful Spanish monarch's eyes.

"Phillip knows that I do what I do for the good of France. Where Spanish and French interests diverge, I will have to serve France. No amount of Spanish gold can change that."

"Henri," I leaned forward to look him directly in the eye. Knowing full well that nothing I said could change his impetuous nature any more than I could successfully do so with my sister, I decided to speak. "I know that you think that you have Phillip and the King balanced well, but you must be careful. Even the weakest of Kings can strike out when you least expect them to. And they may very well prove to be lethal to you."

He gave me a tight smile. "I understand, Sister. That is why I have no desire to start a war with Spain. Wars rarely end the way that we expect them to. I have little desire to spend expensive men on a war with Spain when they can be of better use elsewhere."

I returned to Charles' bedside while Louis met with Guise. I knew that Louis would give me a detailed report of what the two men said, so I was not worried about being excluded from their meeting. To my delight, my son began to babble at me, something that he had not had the strength to do so before.

"Would you like to go back to Nevers, my beautiful boy?" As I watched my son, Guise's warning came to me suddenly. Going to our ducal palace there would separate Louis from us, an idea that I found distasteful after his weeks away from us at St. Germain.

"Can we run up and down the staircase?" The elaborate spiral staircase was irresistible to any child. I understood his desire to play on it as soon as possible. I also understood that if he wanted to play there so badly, it was a sign that he was recovering from his illness.

"I will make a promise to you: if you get well enough to run by New Year's, you may run up and down the stairs as much as you wish." At that, his eyes brightened and for the first time, I had hope that my son would not be taken from me.

At supper, Louis and I dined quietly together, while I waited for him to tell me the details of his meeting with Guise. "He wants me to return to Rome." Louis looked forlorn as he spoke. A trip to the Vatican meant that he would be even further from us.

"Why on earth would he ask you to go to Rome? And would the King allow you to leave so soon?" A departure so quickly after Joyeuse's defection would look suspicious. Now, more than ever, we needed to ally with the King's suspicious nature. As I had warned Guise, even a weak King could strike when we least expected.

"Guise wants me to ask the Pope point blank if the League has the Pope's blessing. Guise worries that without the Pope's support, our fight against the heretics will have little basis. Papal blessing will cause more nobles to flock to our cause without feeling conflicted."

"What will you tell the King? How can you keep him from finding out your true purpose in going to Rome?' Fear for my husband caused my blood to run cold. I had no desire to lose his presence and I was not willing to allow him to place himself in jeopardy with an accusation of treason.

"I will tell the King that I want the Pope's support to succeed to Mantua. I still haven't lost hope that I can manage to do so. I will also tell the King that I will take his case for war against Spain to the Pope. Phillip has had the favor of the Papacy for far too long. It is time that we broke Rome's favoritism towards Spain."

I nodded; Louis' reasoning was solid. "I don't want you to leave France, but if you think that you should do so, then you will go with my blessing." Louis took my hand and squeezed it. If he left me, I would miss him more than I wanted to admit.

With his potential trip to Rome in our minds, we spent Christmas 1584 in Paris together quietly, just the three of us . The only dark spots were the absences of my daughters. While I knew that custom dictated that they live with their future in-laws, I wanted to have all of my children sitting around me. To my delight, Charles continued to recover, taking tentative steps on Christmas Eve that proved to be the best Christmas present that I could have hoped for. I wrote letters to the Queen Mother, Queen Louis and the Guise women thanking them for their prayers and support. Finally, God did not see fit to take my son from me. As New Year's Day dawned, my son burst into our bedchamber and tried to leap onto our bed. The motion woke Louis from a sound sleep and laughing, he tried to admonish Charles for his behavior. As our son climbed into bed between us, we savored the moment that we were together and fortune seemed to be smiling upon us.

"Mama, you promised!" Charles bounded from the carriage and into the frigid January air on his way towards the Ducal palace of Nevers. The promised spiral staircase lured my son in and I had no chance of stopping him before he reached it. There was also no chance of standing on ceremony as the staff of the palace stood before us. While my son screamed and ran up and down the polished stone steps of the staircase, I directed my Parisian maids in settling in for our stay at Nevers.

As soon as I could, I checked my correspondences. I had two letters from Louis, who, for the moment, was with the King at the

Louvre. The King would not give him leave to go to Rome, which meant that he could not aid Guise and the League in their efforts. Unbeknownst to the King, Louis and Guise continued to correspond, with Louis giving Guise advice on the proposed war in the Low Countries. The King planned to send Guise and his army to Antwerp to besiege the city, while my brother-in-law lobbied to change his mind. Guise was forced to appease both Henri and Phillip on an ongoing basis.

"As you warned him, Guise is torn between two royal masters," Louis wrote to me from his apartments at the Louvre. *"If he does not proceed to Antwerp with his men, he defies the King. Phillip's ambassador, Mendoza, has threatened to deliver a copy of the terms Guise submitted to at Joinville if he does attack Antwerp. Guise is paralyzed and he begs for my help if I ever make it to Rome."* Guise had signed the treaty saying that upon the death of Henry III he would accept Spanish troops to promote the Cardinal of Bourbon as heir to France, displacing Navarre. This agreement amounted to treason and showed for all that Guise intrigued with a foreign power behind the King's back. Louis faced the same choice of maintaining his stated loyalty to his King or his secret loyalty to Guise. He asked for my counsel in what to do and I readily gave it to him. I could hear his growing frustration with the vacillating King. Before coming to the throne, Henri III was a decisive soldier, but now, it was a rare occasion when he made *any* decision, good or bad. I hoped that Louis's enormous store of patience never ran out.

I continued my personal policy of finding a middle way, advising Louis to remain at the King's side at the Louvre, advising him alongside Epernon. As long as he stood beside the King each day, he could hardly be suspected of being a traitor. While at the Louvre, he continued to ask the King for permission to depart for Rome to ask for Papal support for the war and for the Dukedom of Mantua. The trip to Rome would take days, during which either Guise or the King could gain the upper hand. Given how recalcitrant the Holy Father proved to be to grant anything to Louis, he could hardly be faulted for the time in which it took to get an answer from the Pope. Once he arrived in Rome my husband would be far away from the looming civil war between the Guise and Valois factions. Hopefully, tucked away in Italy and the French countryside we were both safe from danger.

That February, Catherine began sending my anxious letters, determined to convince me to compel Louis to go to Rome. *"Mendoza showed himself at Joinville, threatening in person to expose my husband to the King. As if he were a naughty boy to be brought before his father for punishment! Without the Guise, Phillip would have no support in France and he well knows it. Henriette, you must prevail upon Louis to take the League's case to the Pope!"* Unwilling to place myself or my husband in the midst of the upcoming fight between Guise and the King, I placed the letter under a pile of papers and promptly went outside for a walk.

By March, the Valois began to cause splinters amongst the Guise and Lorraine cousins, threatening to split their generations old alliance. Christine, Lorraine's eldest daughter, also happened to be the Queen Mother's favorite grandchild and as with the King, she favored this child to the exclusion of all others. Calling on a grandmother's privilege, the Queen Mother called Christine to the Tuileries to wait upon her in person, which gave Catherine de Medici a bargaining chip against the Guise faction. With his beloved daughter ensconced within the Tuileries, Lorraine was all but neutralized and Guise lost one of his most powerful allies.

Heeding the King's wishes and my advice, Louis continued to linger at the Louvre, waiting for a sign that either faction would soon gain the upper hand. Louis wrote me almost daily, reassuring me that he was safe and that he would make no moves to openly support either side. Daily I thanked God that I had heeded Guise's advice and retired to Nevers where I would not be brought into the conflict. In my absence, Montpensier continued to agitate the populace of Paris and speak against the King's alliance with the Protestant Elisabeth of England. Rumors spread across Paris that any extremist priests willing to speak against the king from the pulpit were on the Duchess de Montpensier's payroll.

In April, however, our idyllic existence in Nevers began to dissipate. Even miles away from Paris, rumors reached us that Guise was planning to eschew war with Spain in favor of civil war against the King. Unbeknownst to the Queen Mother or his own daughter, Lorraine accepted Guise's offer of the towns of Metz, Verdun and Toul, marching onto them with the troops earmarked for Antwerp and giving control of the Champagne region of western France directly to Guise. If Guise thought that the King would surrender the towns easily, he was mistaken; Epernon rallied royal troops to Metz and throughout April and May the city held out against Guise's forces. Now there was no doubt that Guise was in open rebellion against the King. This moved far beyond rhetoric; lines would have to be drawn amongst the nobility and choices made.

As soon as I heard of Guise's defeat, I wrote in alarm to Louis. *"Pray that the King does not think that you are loyal to Guise or that you will flock to his banner."* Louis responded by writing that the King spent his days roaming Paris, strengthening the city's fortifications, certain that Guise would turn his well-placed army toward the city that was a short march away.

While the King sent reinforcements to Metz, Guise split his troops in an attempt to incite rebellion across France. Gambling that Catherine de Medici would not harm her favorite grandchild, an emboldened Lorraine went north towards Calais to siege towns across the region and to cut off any supply lines crossing the Channel from England. Suddenly, the King's alliances with the Protestants began to pay dividends as Navarre and his troops were amongst the few loyal troops to come to the aid of the King. Years of consolidating possessions in the north meant, however, that the Guise and Lorraine cousins had a virtual lock in the north and Navarre could not manage to break that lock.

In hindsight, perhaps Guise would have been better served to strengthen his presence in the north and be satisfied with it. A lifelong man of the people, however, Guise assumed that wherever his allies went, so did the support of the people and he began to feel overconfident. The city of Lyon gave itself over to the League

without a shot, disregarding its history as the first city the King visited at the start of his reign. With no encouragement from the League, the people of the city tore down their own citadel and offered the keys to the city to the League. This rebellion was motivated instead by personal grievances. The city's governor, a man named Mandelot, used the rebellion to take revenge upon Epernon for appointing a new loyalist commander at the citadel. .
With Lyon's show of disloyalty to the King's man, the King faced the problem of his subjects openly rebelling against him even without incitement from the League. The uprising showed that remaining favorite of the King could be defeated with the proper motivation. The people were finally punishing him for his partisanship of his newly raised nobodies.

By late March of 1585, the League troops decided to control the southern ports along the Mediterranean, in an effort to control all French ports that were held not by the Protestants. If the League could control the northern and southern coasts of France, they would have a virtual embargo against Spanish and German commerce across the Mediterranean. The temptation of such a dominant position proved to be too much for the League to resist.

To compensate him for his support, the League offered Louis the governorship of Provence, which would make him the most powerful man in southern France. *"As always, I told Guise that the honor would be mine, but I could not openly rebel against the King. If the southern campaign were to fail, the League would need a loyal man in the King's service to negotiate the League's surrender. Guise would not hear of a potential threat, of course, and he scoffed at the idea. I may be portrayed later as a coward, but I believe that by holding to our middle way we will be safest."* Reading those words, I breathed a sigh of relief that Louis continued to honor our pact.

Reassured that Louis had both our best interests in mind, I wrote to my sister and suggested that Louis would be the best ally if the League were to meet with any resistance. I suggested that his diplomatic skills would be the most effective no matter what the outcome.

Now, I thank God that I did so. At the close of March, as Charles bounded in front of me in the palace gardens looking for flowers to pick, a message came to me from Paris. "Madame, the Duc de Nevers asked that you open this at once."

I scanned Louis's letter, which he had hastily scrawled in his own hand. The southern campaign had proven to be a disaster. Overconfident that the King had pulled his troops to Paris to defend the capital, Guise had assumed that Marseille was ripe for the taking. With no large force commanded by Epernon to oppose him, Marseille had few defensive fortifications, only an open port. The League forces marched into the city, ready to "liberate it from heresy." Never a hotbed of Protestant activities, the city looked like an easy victory for the league. One alert merchant, however, gained advance notice that the League was on its way and organized a resistance comprised of Protestant residents to face the men marching upon the city. Just as with Lyon, local resistance decided the battle with little interference from either Royal troops or League forces. Marseille demonstrated that the Protestants could be underestimated, and the League used it as proof that the heretics were better armed than Navarre would have the King believe.

Once he heard of the defeat at Marseille, Louis declined the offer to serve as governor of Provence. *"I have assured Guise that I still hold to the ideals of the League to destroy heresy, and that I only hope this defeat is a temporary setback,"* he wrote to me. *"I must confess, however, that the endless back and forth between the League and the King's troops worries me. I hope that the King will not place me in the battlefield."*

His last sentence worried me. Louis had sustained an injury before our marriage falling from a horse. Thanks to his injuries he walked with a slight limp that excused him from participating in active battle. If the King grew desperate enough, he might force Louis to return to the battlefield. I found another reason to worry as I read the rest of his letter. *"I have been given permission from the King, however, to travel to Rome to present his plans for war to His Holiness. I will also take Guise's case to the Pope."* I groaned at his words, but I continued to scan his letter. *"Before I go to Rome,*

I will have to take on provisions at Nevers. I fully expect our home to be ready for me when I arrive.

My husband was coming home to me. That much reassured me.

Louis had precious few days to spend with us at Nevers and he kissed us both before he began the well-traveled road to Rome. Before he left, he once again assured me that we would make any decisions regarding our loyalties together. "You and I are declared for the King," he told me before striding out of our home and into the crisp courtyard air. "I will make any apologies and excuses to Guise. He knows full well that I am his friend and that he needs me to speak to the King for him in the event of a disaster. Do not worry," he pulled me close and gave me a final kiss. I could smell the leather of his doublet, infused with the warmth from his body. If we stayed outside much longer, he would begin to get cold. "We are on good terms with the League and our position won't harm us."

Reassured, I waved goodbye to him while Charles shouted "Bye, Papa!" at the top of his lungs. I resolved to start disciplining my son for his bad manners, just as soon as I recovered from my fear of losing him.

I moped in my sitting room for the next several days, writing to Guise and Catherine as a devoted sister. Together, we made plans for our late sister's daughter. Each day, I wrote to my own daughters, giving them motherly advice. Letters came from the King, asking for my assurance that I supported him, but unwilling to make a decision without first talking with Louis, I ignored them. With my son beside me, I attended Mass in the cathedral and one hot morning, when we rose to receive Communion, I noticed a sharp-eyed priest eyeing me intently. My suspicions were immediately raised and I felt that I was in the midst of an intrigue. As I had no desire to contemplate any scheming within my own duchy of Nevers, I pointedly ignored the man. Charles and I spent the rest of Sunday at our leisure, sitting as I tried to teach my son his letters.

Early on Monday morning, I heard a discreet throat clearing as I sat at my desk in the castle's study. Looking up, I saw the castle's chamberlain, Monsieur Berou who had served since my father's time, at the doorway.

"Forgive me, My Lady—you have visitors." His expression showed his distaste at his errand, so I guessed that he felt the same distaste for the visitors.

"Who is it?" With any luck, I could shoo them away without any repercussions.

Berou sighed, "It's the Bishop of Nevers, with his secretary."

I let out a loud groan, unconcerned with propriety. "Very well, let them in."

Since our last conversation years ago, I had successfully avoided speaking directly to the Bishop again, leaving the distasteful task to Louis. Since the nomination of Bishops fell to the King, I left the man's official business to the King to handle. Any other business could easily be handled by Louis. Now, unfortunately, he was at my doorstep and I could not avoid him any longer. I stood and walked to the middle of the room in order to receive him.

To my surprise, the man designated as his secretary was the same man who made me feel uneasy at Mass the day before. "Gentlemen, I was unaware that we were to meet today. You must excuse me, my own secretary," I said the last word as I fixed a cold look on the unfamiliar man, "did not tell me that you were waiting for me."

The Bishop spoke up, "I'm afraid, My Lady, that what we have to say to you could not wait. We came at once to speak with you."

My spirits sank at the thought of what they thought so important that they could barge in without invitation. I would not give either man the tactical advantage, however, so I kept my voice level.

"Very well, what is it?'

"Your Ladyship is no doubt aware that the League's forces are shoring up defensive positions across the countryside in order to defend France against the Heretics."

I was unaware of that particular interpretation of the League's activities, but I was curious as to what the man's designs were. "Is

France in danger of invasion from Protestants, Father?"

He tapped his fingertips together, steepling them as if discussing a mundane point of theology. "Alas, yes—Elizabeth of England is flooding the country with Swiss mercenaries and English money. The King of Navarre marches additional troops across the countryside. It is only a matter of time before the two join forces to betray the King and attack France."

"Good Heavens—is the King aware of this? I suppose we are fortunate that Navarre is my own cousin!" My words were laced with sarcasm. His own were fraught with intimidation. If he thought to scare me, he knew very little of me. I suspect that he chose the moment that my husband left me alone with our young son to pounce upon me and scare me into making a rash decision. How little that arrogant toad knew me!

"While you, My Lady, are kinsman to Navarre, your subjects here in Nevers are devoted Catholics. We have no assurances that if the Protestants were to overtake the town that they would not lose their lives. As the spiritual leader of this region, I cannot allow that to happen."

"And just how do you expect to keep that from happening?" I tapped my finger against my cheek, hoping it would cause him to expose more of his plan. He had proven earlier to be rash and arrogant enough in our earlier meeting. I was certain that he had changed little in the past few years.

"The people are ready to defend themselves." The priest beside him spoke simply. It was the first time I heard the man's voice and I immediately did not like it. It sounded menacing and I could hear the threat behind his words.

"What people? Defend how? Are you speaking of *my* people, Father?" Were they stupid enough to incite open rebellion against Louis and myself? Fear tugged at me, but years of intrigue at the court meant that I knew too well how to hide my feelings.

"Madame, France is beset by enemies and if the King is unable to protect his subjects, then they have every right to defend themselves." The priest stood and strode towards me in an attempt to frighten me into submission. I would not bend to his manipulations, however.

"It appears to me, Father—what is you name, Father?" Fixing the most haughty stare I could manage on the man, I stared him down.

"Thomas, M'lady. I am Father Thomas."

"I see, thank you, Father Thomas. It is ever so reassuring to know the names of the men who visit my home. Now, Father Thomas—it appears as if you are creating a crisis where there is none. None of the Protestant troops are stationed anywhere near Nevers, nor have they made any attempts to attack us. The last I heard from Paris, all troops are awaiting the siege of Antwerp, not of Paris."

"For the time being, My Lady, the focus is on the Low Countries. But the League is concerned with what these foreign troops will do once the siege is over." The bishop spread his fingers and adopted a condescending tone. Had he thought to subdue me, he was wrong. Why was France cursed with so many officious blowhards in church offices? Bourbon was bad enough, but now I was forced to endure a second man with pretensions of superiority sitting directly across from me.

"Are not the Jesuits aligned with the League? Father Thomas, you have the look of a Jesuit." My rage was building, frightening the two of them. For a second, Father Thomas' face blanched.

"Of course, we share the League's desire that heresy be eradicated. We have a directive from Rome to protect the sanctity of the Holy Church."

"And the League is headed by the Duc de Guise, who has so far not communicated to me that Nevers is in any danger. In fact," I tilted my head to the side, "I don't remember Guise stating anything of the sort for weeks. Perhaps you are worried about nothing, gentlemen."

Both men started to speak, but the Bishop cut the priest off. "Father Thomas and I are concerned with the survival of our Holy Church. While we would not presume to have the grasp of French political issues that His Majesty possesses, we are sworn to defend the Church and its faithful congregants."

"My Lord the Duc de Guise has sworn to the Pope, the King and myself that he will not act in any way without His Holiness' permission. And Guise will not take up arms against the King. As a Bishop of the church, it is your duty to obey the will of the Pope, is it not?"

The Bishop nodded, "Certainly, my lady."

"And as Guise has received no instruction from either his masters to arm towns such as Nevers, doing so would be in violation of your duty to the Church, would it not?"

The Bishop continued to sputter a response, but I held up my hand, interrupting him. "What I have heard from the two of you, gentlemen, is that you support a rebellion against the King and the League. And that is deeply troubling to me." I rose and strode to my desk, while propriety forced both men to their feet once I was standing. Placing my palms flat on the desk in front of me, I looked at both of them, daring them to contradict my reasoning.

"The will of the populace, however, is not so easy to ascertain. As a man of the cloth, it is our responsibility to lead them to prudent acts."

"But what you have told me today, is that you feel it prudent to lead them in open rebellion against their temporal and spiritual masters. As a Catholic in good standing, that horrifies me."

"Dangers surround us, Madame. The Enemy uses his wiles to separate us from the truth. At any moment, any of us could be at risk from Satan's treachery." Father Thomas' eyes darted around the room and I knew at once that he was threatening my son. My maternal instinct leapt to protect Charles.

"If 'Satan' dares to come into this home, I can assure you that he will find this home well-armed. That applies to our spiritual warfare as well as our physical ones." I swallowed down the horror I felt at the threat against my son. "And may I remind you both that my husband, the Duc de Nevers, is the King's loyal subject as am I. We will both take arms to defend the King's interests. The same applies to all of the people under our rule. Anyone who attempts to do otherwise will face the King's justice." I stared them down for several moments.

Finally, the Bishop found his voice, "I pray that you and your family remain safe in God's hands."

I would hear no more. Striding towards the door, I threw it open, ready to scream for Berou. To my relief, I found him sitting in a bench in the hallway outside of the study. "Madame," he bowed to me. I thanked God for the man's discreet loyalty.

"These men are just leaving. Please escort them to the courtyard." He gave me a curt nod and ushered the men out of the house.

The second the horrible men left, I grabbed pen and paper and began scribbling a note to the King. *"Cousin, never doubt that you have my unwavering love and loyalty, Henriette de Nevers."* At Berou's reappearance at the door, I handed the folded letter to him. "Find a man you trust and instruct him to deliver this to the Louvre immediately. He is not to stop for anything until this is in the King's own hand."

My next act was to write a hasty note to Guise, warning him of the Jesuit's duplicitous behavior.... *"Bewarned that Nevers harbors traitors, traitors to the King who would betray all of His loyal subjects."* Guise was clever enough to understand my warning and if the letter was intercepted, it was inoffensive enough to sound suspect. Berou sent the missive to Guise's headquarters on the Marne River outside Paris and I prayed that it arrived before the conspirators could act against Guise.

My hands shaking, I then penned a letter to Louis, warning him of the threat spoken against Charles' life. I added that Louis should advise the Pope that some Catholics were acting independently of Guise and the King, which made Papal blessing of the League that more important. Without written instructions from Rome, Catholics were making plans on their own.

May passed agonizingly slow for me. With Berou's help, I recruited as many of Louis's loyal men as possible to guard the Ducal palace of Nevers. I had no desire to sit behind a fortified citadel, but the threat against my son made my caution necessary. Faced with few options, I continued to send letters to the Queen Mother at the Tuileries, assuring her of our loyalty and warning her of the conspiracies across France. Safeguarded by trusted men, the letters flew across the countryside as I did as much as I could to keep my son and myself safe.

Days after my missive to the King, I received a response, full of his gratitude for my and Louis' loyalty to the crown. Now more than ever, the King needed allies as even he and Epernon were becoming estranged. The two quarreled openly in the King's chambers over the decision to face the League directly or to continue to play the King's waiting game. Louis's stated loyalty was more valuable to the King than ever.

Louis wrote from Rome to reassure me that the men guarding the palace would keep Charles and myself safe. Luckily, the weather continued to be cold and rainy, which meant my boisterous son had little desire to go outside to play. We spent our days together playing as I kept a watchful eye over every servant who waited upon him. If I was in any danger myself, I was not aware of it. My concern was only for my remaining son and heir.

Guise wrote to me, confessing that rebellions against the leaders of the League were beginning to break out all over France. *"Sadly, that is the cost of inactivity. Soldiers sit around, doing virtually nothing. The populace see them and imagine that they are there to take their aggression out on them."* On Louis' advice, I offered no advice or words of support to Guise, in case my letters to him were being read by Royalist spies. After telling Louis about my last short warning to Guise, he decided that I should remain more cautious in my wordings when writing to my brother-in-law.

My sister Catherine, however, showed no such restraint. With the Queen Mother shuttered away in the Tuileries, she was free to continue in the Parisian salons that spoke out against the King and his Protestant allies. She filled me in on all of the gossip from Paris and maneuvering of the court. Thanks to my sister and her pen, I missed virtually nothing of the court's goings on. The King, she complained, sat and dallied, making no plans against Spain and none to answer to the League's advances. While Guise and the Duc de Lorraine continued to win more towns for the League, the King continued to quarrel with Epernon over his strategy. "The hero of

Jarnac, the man who made war for his brother, now does nothing once he himself sits on the throne."

April brought with it a tide of League victories. While the King searched in vain for money and a loyal Catholic noble to fight for his side, Guise continued to rally more of the common people to his side. In mid-April, Caen and Orleans belonged to the League. Normandy was virtually an independent duchy governed by Guise. I was plagued by nightmares of priests with bloodstained eyes coming towards me, attacking me in my bed. In those dreams, I cried out for Charles but I could never hear his voice. Upon waking, I ran to his bedroom to see if he was safe.

Berou found a young man loitering in the garden behind the Ducal palace. When he told me, I felt a chill. Was he sent by Father Thomas to terrorize me? Was it an innocent man, who simply wandered too far onto our property? Was it a warning? I spent the entire night racked with fear and praying for Louis to return to us.

Warm weather returned to Nevers and I could only look at the buds bursting on the trees outside of my bedchamber window. A cold has sapped every last bit of my energy. What worry has not done to me, this sickness has accomplished. I spend most of my days sleeping, determined to get well as soon as possible. My illness forced me to leave Charles's care into his nurse's hands. Berou visits me when he can, during the moments when I am conscious and up to seeing visitors.
He has learned that there is a large cell of Jesuits in Gien who plan to march towards Guise's headquarters and join the League. According to his intelligence, they are aided by the Jesuits and the Signeor of Gien.
I seethe, feeling incompetent at the fact that I have been laid low by my sickness. The moment Louis returns to Nevers, we will dismiss the Sigenor of Gien and banish the Jesuits from our lands. I have no patience for anyone who acts independently of both King and the League.

That Sunday, as the parishioners of Nevers gathered for Mass, the priest of the cathedral spoke of the need for unity amongst loyal Catholics. He did so with a sizable contribution from me and the priests agreed to continue speaking out against the rebellion to the east in Gien. I hope that this rebellion is contained in the village, but I can do very little now while my body is racked with fever.

Today, I finally found the strength to pull myself out of bed and return to the running of the household. Most of the staff were either like Berou, lifelong retainers of the Cleves family, or our servants who came with us from Paris. Charles' nurse is one of those who followed me from Paris and he has known her his entire life. Claude Catherine sent her to me, insisting that the woman who raised her own children was the best choice for safeguarding my son.

As I haltingly went through the motions of my duties, Berou walked into my study. Neither of us had ever stood on ceremony, but the ashen look on his face told me that this was no time to obey the laws of etiquette.

He could not speak and as I clenched the paper in my hand so tightly that I tore it, I could only look up at him wordlessly. "Whatever you have to say, I do not want to hear it."

He shook his head, "I'm sorry, My Lady. I must tell you this. It's your son."

I let out a primal scream, one that broke my heart and likely his eardrums. My hands fisted at my hairline, and I began to rock in my chair.

"His nurse was walking him in the gardens. It's been so warm out that I agreed that it would be good for him to get the fresh air. When I realized that they had been gone for over two hours, I went to check on them. I found her body shoved against the hedges."

"No, no, no, no, no, no! You will not tell me this! I will not listen to you! How dare you sprout this nonsense to me?"

"My Lady, we did not find his body. We did find a note. He has been kidnapped and the perpetuators left this note." He handed it to me and I stared at it as if it were a wasp that might bite me.

Moments before, I thought that my son was lost forever. Now I struggled to understand the meaning of what he told me. Someone had taken my son and they were presumptuous enough to write to me. Although I wanted as little to do with the note, I had to act quickly in order to save my child. With strength that only a mother in terror for her child's life possesses, I snatched the offending scrap of paper and scanned its contents.

"The price of non-action is steep, particularly during these times of heresy. As our lord the Duc de Nevers has resisted the call to take arms against the Protestants threatening our borders, we have been forced to act. Once you and your husband act in favor of the League and its Holy duty, your son will be returned to you. Ignore us and the boy may well come to harm."

I looked at Berou, who had dedicated his life to keeping our family safe. There was no man in Nevers that I trusted more. "Help me, what should I do?"

He took a seat in front of me, weighing my options. "I won't lie to you, Madame. The Jesuits are well-armed and have been training for years for a fight. If we go looking for the boy, we will meet a well-armed resistance."

"And which men should I send in, loyal troops or ones who side with the League?" Even in the most personal decisions, one must choose a side. This was what France had come to.

"Your best bet is to appeal to Guise to send League allied men. If the King sends in troops they'd likely be cut down. Then, you will have an additional problem of being accused of having an open rebellion on your own domains. I think that you should not involve the King's troops in this."

"All right, then what do you suggest I do?"

"Let me use my men. I have a few here and in Gien who may be able to help."

The King has finally decided to act, but this time, he has done so in the most inappropriate way. He has ordered a detachment of his Swiss Guards to Nevers as a favor to Louis for his loyalty. I could only laugh at the irony that the King would act at the moment we least need him to do so. How he heard of my situation was beyond me, but it demonstrated that the King had spies very close to me. I must be more cautious than even Louis and I had suspected.

Once I received word that the troops were headed to Nevers, I wrote immediately to the King, thanking him for his quick action but warning him that the men who had my son were extremists, likely to act in a lethal manner once they saw Royalist troops headed their way.

The King would not hear of it, stressing that he was acting in a way that would protect my house and my lands. Once the troops arrived, Nevers became occupied territory and the kidnappers were driven underground. They also forced Berou's operatives to chase down little more than dead ends as they prowled the countryside for information.

Louis wrote to me to say that he has pressured Guise to get his own house in order. *"The rebellion that you have fermented is now splintering. My son is now the victim of the League's infighting."* Louis added that Guise was quite put out at how bluntly he spoke to him, but my husband spoke as a father, not an ally.

Louis had hoped that his candor would convince Guise to send men to root out the Jesuit extremists, but Guise dragged his feet in response. Helpless in Rome, Louis could only write angry letters and do his best to fend off the King and his well-intentioned offers of more armed men.

The body of a young boy was discovered floating in the Loire. I refused to believe that it was Charles. I would not even go to identify the body, instead sending Berou to do the task for me. As Berou's portly wife sat beside me, comforting me, I prayed prayers that I feared God would not listen to. He has rarely listened to my prayers, so why would now be any different?

Berou returned shortly after lunch. With his wife's arms encircling me like a steel trap, he walked into my bedchamber. "It's not you son, Milady. It was an apprentice boatman who fell off of a barge a few days ago. Your son is likely still alive." I collapsed into tears; at least this time, God *did* consider my prayers.

I have just sent a letter to Anna d'Este, demanding that her son honor our loyalty and send men to aid us in our search for Charles. Guise might ignore me, but a mother's pleas are another thing.

Two days later, a group of men burst into my study, all of them dusty from the road. Before I could dress them down for their interruption, they removed their cloaks and I saw that they were Jesuit priests. "The Duchess of Nemours sent us. We are here to aid in your search for your son, My Lady."
I called for Berou and by supper, we had a plan. The priests were to infiltrate the Jesuit community in Gien, and while there, gain any information about my son's whereabouts. "If you learn that his is dead, please let me know. The agony of not knowing his fate is much worse."

In May, the Cardinal de Bourbon, "Petite Homme," who Guise put forth as an alternative to Navarre, took it upon himself to write a declaration stating that he was the King's most loyal subject and that the League only sought to stamp out heresy. While these were fine sentiments and not unlike own my correspondence with the King, Bourbon did so without first consulting Guise. The puppet began to pull his own strings, due in part to his fear that the Queen Mother would have his pointed head upon a pike.
Unfortunately, as was common with my uncle Bourbon, his mouth outpaced his common sense. Almost as soon as he published his statement, he began preaching against the mismanagement of funds by the Crown, angering the King. His proclamation caused deeper splits between the League factions. I felt relief that the men sent to rescue my son were not Guise men but fellow Jesuits. God willing, Charles would be returned to me before the League imploded. I had no desire for my son to be used as a pawn any longer.

I have heard from the Jesuits in Gien, who give me good news. Charles is being held in a modest home outside of the village of Perroy. "He's been treated well, but under close guard." Apparently, my son had been sick, the stress too much for him. Although I'm relieved to hear that his is safe, I am furious at the idea that he had to convalesce without me to care for him.

With the beginning of June, the number of towns under League and not Royal control could not be ignored. While her son would do nothing to secure his throne, the Queen Mother made steps to negotiate with Guise. To that end, she rode to Chalons-sur-Marne to open talks to reconcile the League with the throne. Anna, Guise's mother and the Queen Mother's lifelong friend, rode alongside the Queen Mother, as did my sister, Catherine. At her side was Christine of Lorraine, who as we suspected was never at any risk of ill treatment from her doting grandmother. When the Queen Mother arrived to negotiate with Guise, she did so with a large contingent of Guise women. This did not bode well for the Valois.

At sixty-five-years old, Catherine de Medici had decades of political activity behind her. No woman in France was more qualified to speak with the League and the King had no more dedicated advocate. Still, Guise's poise that summer astounded the Queen Mother. Guise knew that he had a distinct advantage over the Valois and he did not hesitate to press that advantage. I cared little for the back and forth between the two. All that I cared about was getting my son returned to me safely.

"Now is the time to make our move," Berou confessed to me at the end of June. We had all grown weary of the anxiety we felt over Charles' disappearance. Louis's patience was frayed and he felt helpless to resolve the situation from Rome. I was determined to make a move as soon as possible. Had I had Louis by my side, I might have been more prudent.

The men who held my son hostage were going north to join Guise to try to influence the terms of the proposed peace treaty between

Guise and the King. With their numbers depleted, it would be easier to find my son and safely bring him home from Perroy. If Berou was unsuccessful, I do not know if a cease fire between Guise and the King would do anything to change their extremist tactics. Desperation began to set in and I sent Berou to discreetly roam the streets of Perroy to offer a financial incentive to end this standoff.

It is the first of July and the heat did nothing more than annoy me as I looked out my study window and onto the courtyard below. Berou has been due for hours, but there is no sign of life on the horizon or the cobblestones below. A thousand different scenarios play inside my head. I am beset with anxiety. I should have insisted that Berou's wife sit with me once again.

To distract me, I open random books in the study, seeing nothing when I looked at them. In my annoyance, I snapped each of them closed, not caring if I hurt the leather spines. In fact, the sharp noise made me feel somewhat better. I smirked at the books in a childish triumph as I heard a noise behind me.

I whirled around to see Berou, who held my son in his arms. I screamed and ran to take Charles into my own arms. Covering him with kisses, I am unable to do anything else for several minutes.

Finally, I turn to the man who returned my life to me. "How?"

He smiled, "It wasn't easy."

The terms of the Treaty of Nemours were a virtual capitulation of the King to the League. Guise became Grand Marshall of the French army, commanding all forces in the kingdom. In addition, the King agreed to appoint only generals approved by Guise. My bother-in-law was now the head of France's army in all but name. Yet as audacious as those terms were, those that dealt with the Protestants were even harsher. All Protestants were to be immediately expelled from France and their property to be immediately seized. As a "concession" they had a year to sell those lands, which would eventually go at a deep discount to Catholics. No Protestant could inherit land, which meant that my niece could not inherit any land from her father, the Prince de Conde. I thanked God that her title Marquess d'Isles came through my sister, who died a Catholic in good standing.

It was just as well, since I doubt Conde even remembered that he had a daughter. The last I had heard from him, Navarre was determined to marry him to a wealthy Protestant heiress. Our decision to place little Catherine in Joinville once again proved to be a wise one.

When Louis heard the terms of the treaty, he was astounded. Wracked with guilt that he could not be there to advise Guise or the King, he nonetheless presented the treaty to the Pope. For once, His Holiness saw fit to receive my husband immediately. When Louis told him of the terms, the Pope told him simply that he was astounded that the King capitulated to this rebellion, "and that the rebels were able to get the King to agree that the rebellion was done in his name."

Louis wrote me to tell me that his visit to Rome was a mistake, especially given how much he was needed in France. He confessed to me that considering how harsh the League's terms were, he could no longer in good conscious support them. *"After much soul searching, I have come to the conclusion that the League violates the Divine Right of kings, of all sovereigns. I cannot support a confederacy that openly flaunts that right."*

By the end of July, the King signed the treaty, announcing its ratification as the oppressive heat of Summer spread over Paris. Epernon urged him to sign it quickly, fearing that the League would make Epernon's exile from France an additional term to the treaty. This signaled a reconciliation between the King and his remaining favorite, but it also meant that Epernon continued to exert too much influence over the King's decision making.

Taking advantage of the King's shrinking allies, Louis obtained his permission to retire from his presence. With the heat of summer and the annual threat of plague coming on, my husband was coming home to Nevers. As Louis galloped north to France, my imbecilic uncle, the Cardinal de Bourbon, did all that he could to unravel the League's gains. Likely prompted by the Queen Mother, he immediately set to soften the terms of the Treaty of Nemours. I pitied Guise for the headaches that the man would continue to cause him in the future. For the moment, the ramifications of the treaty meant that Louis and I could afford to step back from public service without sacrificing our own loyalties.

"I'm sorry to force you out in this heat." Louis looked at the sweat pooling at my brow. I self-consciously dabbed at it, while Charles tugged at my skirt. I let go of his tiny hand and he ran towards his father. Louis scooped him up and covered his face with kisses.

"I can easily bear it now that you're here. I suppose it's better than the heat in Rome." I smiled up at him.

"I would wish that it was quieter here than in Rome." He pursed his lips. I was grateful that he was now home to help me deal with the threat of an uprising. Working together as a team, we were better equipped to handle it with his threat.

"I wish that this was the end of the struggle between the King and the League." Despite the fact that it was his homecoming, we would always speak openly to one another.

"Darling, I doubt that it will be resolved anytime soon." Guise's treaty bought us some much needed time to discuss our next move. God willing, we would have enough time to consider our options before we were pressed to make a hasty decision.

"Luckily, I have the two of you to occupy my time." Charles wiggled in his arms and Louis hugged him even closer to his body. We walked into the palace, with Charles between us. Although I would prefer that we were five strong, I knew that my daughters were safe and so were their futures. Returned to me and in full health, Charles' future looked bright as well. As for husband and I, we were determined to spend the next days united in mind and united in body.

Historical Note

Unlike her youngest sister, Marie, Henriette led a long life and her descendants would later rule Poland, Mantua, and France. In Lady of the Court, I portray her as desperate to hold onto her status, and I think that her many descendants would show that she succeeded beyond her own expectations.

My own perception of Henriette changed after I began researching her. After seeing the 1994 version of Queen Margot, I assumed that she spent her life from one affair to another. She certainly is depicted in the film as being even more sensual than Margot herself. Surprisingly, there is no record of her having an affair outside of her well-documented one with Coconnas. Did she enter that liaison as a way to cope with the loss of her son? I couldn't find any hard evidence that she did, but it seemed plausible for a woman in deep mourning.

Charles I, Duc de Nevers and later Duke of Mantua was never involved in a kidnapping plot. That bit came out of my imagination. It is the only deviation I took from established historical fact in *Lady of the Court.*

Laura du Pre

A Preview of Fate's Mistress
Hotel de Guise, Paris, January 1586

"Henri, for God's sake—slow down! I cannot keep up. My legs are too short!" I watched as my husband's wide shoulders trailed down the hallway before me, his enraged voice booming from the thick, stone walls. I scurried behind him, doing my best to keep pace with him. When he was in one of his rages, there was no reasoning with him. Yet, that fact had never stopped me before. I was in the third month of my latest pregnancy, my twelfth, and could still scamper behind my husband.

His hulking legs continued to put him further away from me, taking one step to match my two. I was far from the shortest woman at court, but Henri, the Duc de Guise, was a giant of a man. No man in France could measure up to his height, the blond giant towered over every man at court. Unfortunately for me, he had a personality to match his oversized body.

"Henri!" I screeched at the top of my lungs, taking my turn in the game that we had perfected in the almost two decades of our marriage. Neither of us would fit a priest's view of a Godly or virtuous man or woman, but then, neither of us had made an effort to pretend that we were anything other than what we were. This arrangement made it easy to be honest with one another. Of course, our determination to be ourselves frequently meant that we found ourselves in screaming matches with one another, but on this one occasion, I was not the person who had enraged my hulking husband.

The person in question was his August Majesty, King Henri III of France, Duc d' Anjou and only surviving son of Catherine de Medici. Last summer, my husband and his Catholic League had successfully compelled the King to agree to place him in charge of the armies of France. My husband immediately appointed his younger brother, the Duc de Mayenne to attack the Protestants that swarmed across France. When the terms were set in the heat of summer, we breathed a sigh of relief that the King had finally come to his senses and decided to protect France from invasion and the threat of heresy from the Protestant Queen of England and my heretic cousin, the King of Navarre.

Today, however, my husband received word from his spies in Normandy that the King had spent the last three months in secret negotiations with the Protestants behind his back. All of the work that Mayenne did on the battlefield was for nothing. Worse still, the King casually broke his promise to the Guise brothers to follow their advice in leading the armies of France.

I continued to try to catch up with him, but he stormed out of the front door of our house and onto the courtyard below, where a saddled horse always waited for him. Watching him so, I seethed. I knew where he was going. He was going to see that strumpet.

Do not misunderstand me—I am no moralist who chafes at the idea of a philandering husband. I have had my own share of lovers myself. I am too lively to be satisfied with a single man, even if that man is my husband; even if he is arguably the most handsome man at court. I have never begrudged Henri for his mistresses as he has rarely objected to my lovers. I object to the idea that he is going to take out his frustration with another woman, while blatantly ignoring me. I have spent too many years in service to the Guise family to be shut out today.

I storm back to my own rooms, passing one of the many retainers who have sworn loyalty to the Guise and the Catholic League. Our cavernous home, the Hotel de Guise, purchased by the previous duke and my mother-in-law, has more than enough room to house the people necessary to sustain a rebellion. Every person in this house has been party to the seditious acts against the King and his favorites. As one of my husband's most ardent allies, I do not take well to being shut out of his council.

Once at my desk, I pulled out pen and paper and began composing letters to allies across France. My husband might not want to acknowledge my usefulness to the League, but there were numerous people who would. After he finished having his sport in bed, we would have words.

* * *

"Every time that I think Henri Valois cannot sink any further, he manages to surprise me!" My sister-in-law, the widowed Duchess de Montpensier, sat her wine on the table before her, careful not to spill any on the intricate lace cloth before her. Her wording was deliberate; while the rest of us still continued to refer to the man on the throne of France as the King, she insisted on insulting him by referring to him as "Henri Valois" as if he were an ordinary citizen. If Montpensier had her way, he would soon become an ordinary citizen. Amongst the noblewomen who ran the female contingent of the League, she was the most ardent. There was no moderation in her tone or in her actions. If she ran the League, Catherine of Lorraine would gladly march upon the Louvre and burn the King in his bed as he slept.

"You would think that for his own survival, he would occasionally take advice from someone other than that useless fop Epernon." As soon as the man's name was out of my mouth, I ground my teeth. Epernon enjoyed the place that rightfully belonged to my husband and the members of the Guise and Lorraine families. As the highest-ranking nobles of France, their place was at the King's hand. Yet, Henri III had decided raise up virtual peasants to the lucrative posts that kept the nobles from going into virtual bankruptcy. Far too many of our retainers and allies had been forced to sell land and assets to make up for the loss of offices that were rightfully theirs.

"If he had a bit of common sense," she absentmindedly picked at the ruffs at her wrists, "he would listen more to your brother-in-law." I groaned inwardly at her accusation. My brother-in-law was the man who had risen with the King's ascension to the throne; and a man who had long-served the Valois kings of France. Louis Gonzaga, who took over my father's title of Duc de Nevers by marrying my older sister, was the only voice of reason left in the King's Privy Chamber. Louis' continued presence there gave us hope that eventually he would get through to the King. Yet, judging by the King's past decisions, he would probably ignore Louis as soon as Epernon whispered into his royal ear.

I shook my head, "I never know what is in Louis' mind. I know that part of him agrees passionately with the League. He is as loyal a Catholic as we are. Yet, he is determined to remain as neutral as he can. It's as if he's terrified to stand up and make a decision."

She shrugged, "Then, speak to Henriette. She is your sister, after all." *I can no more control my sister than my husband can control his*, I thought, as I avoided Montpensier's gaze. As controlling as the woman who sat before me was, Henriette was just as nebulous. I never knew her mind either. Sometimes, I felt as if my sister was a cold, calculating fish.

"My relationship with my sister is complicated and the King himself made it so." Henriette once was the most senior woman of the Queen's household, as well-placed in the King's court as her husband. In a characteristically stupid move, however, the King decided one evening to trap my sister in a fake affair and "expose" her before the court. She fled from the court in humiliation and has barely made any effort to return. If I wish to see her, I usually have to drop by the Hotel de Nevers and make a sisterly visit. Even though it is selfish, I am very put out by her self-imposed exile from court. Without her, I have few real friends to rely upon, save my radical sister-in-law. Montpensier is quite a handful, angrily railing against the King at every opportunity. I count myself as a radical, but her extremism gets on my nerves on a regular basis.

"Catherine, you mentioned the new printing blocks—would you show them to me?"

She clapped her hands. "Of course! I was afraid you would never ask. Come!" Standing, she pulled me up from my chair and dragged me outside as I struggled to put on my heavy cape. The damp cold settled on Paris this time of year, bringing with it a heavy fog over the river. With an almost gleeful bounce to her step, she led me to the stables of her Hotel de Guise and at an empty stall, she glanced both ways and opened the padlock.

"Here they are." The carvers finished just last week. They were well-paid for their silence." Throwing back a horse blanket, she showed the wooden printing blocks to me. One of them depicted the King of France as a priest, shorn of his hair and shorn of his crown. "The price of betrayal of Gaul" the inscription screamed in bold lettering. Another featured a Protestant army, marching upon the familiar walls of Paris, with babies hanging aloft on pikes. I glanced at Montpensier, "Isn't that a bit much?" My stomach lurched at the sight and the wave of nausea caused by my pregnancy.

"Innocents suffer in war, and if the Protestants and their mercenaries from Germany and Switzerland are allowed to march across France, there is no telling what horrors the city will endure. It is best that we acknowledge the danger and do something before this image comes true!" Her eyes shone with the passion of a fanatic. In those brown depths, I saw a touch of madness. Still, I knew that I had few friends and allies in Paris, and given how Henri had pushed me away a few days before, I could not afford to alienate his sister. Instead, I turned to look at another plate.

"This one doesn't have an image," I frowned, trying to make sense of it. She made a reverse nod, acknowledging my confusion.

"This is blank so that we can create pamphlets from it. The lines are there to make the sentences straight. Here," she rummaged around in the hay until she found a small sack, "are the individual letters that the printers will use to make the pamphlets. The beauty of this, is that we can use any number of combinations of letters. We can make several different pamphlets and we can do it quickly."

"And are you absolutely certain that you want them taken from your house? At least there, you can have complete control over the printing process." Something told me that the wooden blocks in front of me were a portent of trouble, but I did not know just how troublesome they would later prove to be. For the moment, my main objection, was the added activity that they would bring to my home.

She shrugged, "Henri promised. As I am a widow, it would not do for me to be seen instigating rebellion against the King's policies." My mouth snapped open in shock. Was she serious? There was no woman in Paris better known for instigating and fermenting rebellion against the King! Why would she bother to stop now? Had she finally realized that she had gone too far? Did she know that the blocks were too dangerous? Yes, there was a chance that her sex would cause the King to have mercy on her if the blocks were found at her home, but it was not a given. She faced just as much danger as the rest of us.

Still, I was determined to demonstrate my usefulness to my husband. Having control of the words printed by the League across the city of Paris, did carry with it an irresistible amount of power. Despite my earlier sense of foreboding, I turned to her.

"I'll see that Philobert finds a place for him at the Hotel de Guise." At least inside my home, they would be under my control. I would see to that.

* * *

Life at the court was very taxing for me. Since 1579, my husband and the King openly quarreled, and the King constantly took pains to make little insults towards my husband and every member of his family. Once the two were playmates, a reflection of the vaunted position that the Guise and my mother-in-law, a granddaughter of a king, enjoyed at court. Soon after the King came to the throne, however, he allowed other men to poison his once close friendship with my husband.

Never at a loss for ambitious men to fawn over him, the King had selected a man named Quelus and another, Charles de Balsac sieur d'Entragues. as his particular favorites in the fashionable sport of dueling. This dueling was not a method of satisfying honor, more a form of playacting to amuse the King and his close friends. Having the King's favor made more than one man reckless, none more so than Quelus. The men were stupid enough to engage in a duel, killing both of them. For his part, the King mourned Quelus to such an extent that the city came out in droves to mock him. d'Entragues sought and received sanctuary at the Hotel de Guise. Thinking that he was doing his old friend a favor, my husband readily tended to the King's favorite, working in vain to keep the man alive, despite his injuries. To our horror, the King turned on both d'Entragues and my husband.

Demanding the body of d'Entragues, the King raged against my husband, accusing him of rebellion against him. When my flabbergasted husband replied that he was doing the King's will, the King went to even more extremes. He stated that d'Entragues came to our home because he was carrying on an affair with me and he sought my aid. I have never been completely faithful to my husband, but even I would never be desperate enough to lie with one of those effeminate favorites. I would sooner lie with a peasant from the fields of Navarre. My husband did not fall for the ruse and buried the man without releasing his body to the King. From that point on, we became a continuous target for the King's ire.

As if this ongoing unpleasantness were not enough, there are enough base individuals at court to make me question the standards of the court. At the forefront of these individuals, is the woman I know to be my husband's current mistress.

Charlotte de Beaune-Semblancy is nothing more than the descendent daughter of a silversmith and the great-granddaughter of a known traitor. By her first marriage, she became Baroness de Sauve. By her second marriage, she had finally ascended to the nobility to become the Marquise de Noirmoutier. She is coarse and without any breeding at all. Every time I am forced to see her, I feel the bile rising up in my mouth.

It is easy to blame my hatred of the woman on her common origins. Yet, I have many more reasons to hate her. She is the Queen Mother's creature, one of her Flying Squadron who spend their days and evenings in various men's beds, coyly plying information from them at the Queen Mother's behest. While most women at court choose their bedfellows for passion or for sport, these women do it for money. Charlotte is one of Catherine de Medici's most accomplished whores, managing the feat of juggling two lovers at once. Even in France, that was quite a task. At her mistresses' command, she jumped between the beds of my cousin, the King of Navarre, and the King's younger brother and heir, until she had alienated the men to a degree that they barely trusted one another. I blame her for alienating them from the King's youngest sister and my own sister, Henriette's close friend, Queen Margot of Navarre. Thanks to Charlotte's machinations, Margot was stripped of her allies at court and left with few friends at court, save my sister.

This behavior was despicable enough, but no act is too shameful for that Circe. I hold Charlotte directly responsible for breaking my sister's heart over a decade ago. While Henriette mourned the sudden death of her only son, she found solace in the arms of a lover. Charlotte schemed to find evidence that sent Henriette's lover to his death. My poor sister was forced to endure those losses within a month of one another, at the time when I thought she might die as well of heartbreak. For these reasons and more, I have no reservations in admitting my hatred of Charlotte.

As I attended the Queen Mother, I kept a wary eye out for Charlotte. I was in no mood to deal with the snake. "Madame de Guise, please hand me my ruff," the Queen Mother gestured to me and I moved forward.

"Here, your Majesty." I spread my hands over the foamy folds, doing my best to straighten them so that they would sit high around her fleshy neck. The Queen Mother nodded her approval of my efforts and I stepped back from her.

"Someone is missing," I heard a sly voice whisper behind me. It was one of the sharp-tongued Mademoiselles. Most of the women my age and older in the Queen's household knew better than to engage in gossip directly in front of her. She publicly decries any hint of scandal, while meeting with her Squadron behind closed doors. It is one of the many hypocrisies that Catherine de Medici has created during her long years at the French court.

"It's Madame de Noirmoutier.! I wonder where she is!" A giggle spilled out from a mouth behind me and I fought the urge to turn around and slap the offender.

"I think it's better to ask where she's been!" This time, the laughter is louder, drawing the Queen's annoyance.

"If you girls have anything to say, I suggest you say it out loud so that we can all hear. No?   Then, I suppose you are simply gossiping. That is a sin and you are both to go to confession to absolve yourselves of your sin." Catherine's words were directed at the two offenders and I was quite impressed at her ability to hear. Craning my neck around to witness their humiliation, I saw one of the girls' mouths snap open. The other girl only blushed furiously. Wordlessly, they both curtsied and made their escape from the Queen Mother's privy chamber.

* * *

I was mercifully spared Charlotte's presence until that afternoon, as the ladies of the Queen Mother's retinue sat and played cards. I exhaled loudly, annoyed as she floated into the room and made her reverence to the Queen. "Forgive me, Madame. My son is sick and I was called to tend to him."

Catherine searched her face, as if looking to detect a lie. "I will pray for your son's health. See that it does not happen again, Madame de Noirmoutier." The Queen Mother's behavior surprised me; was Charlotte acting independently of her Mistress' instructions?

Like the other ladies of the court, I was smart enough to know not to openly quarrel with Charlotte, which meant that I was forced to be civil to her in the Queen Mother's presence. Away from the sharp eyes of Catherine de Medici, however, the woman was fair game. I would have to bide my time. Spying my mother-in-law across the chamber, I rose and took a seat next to her. She was reading a book in Italian. Like the Queen Mother, she was an Italian and they often spoke in their native language to alleviate their homesickness. While I could speak and read Italian, I was far from a native speaker.

"What are you reading?" I gazed over at Anna d' Este, the Dowager Duchess de Guise and Nemours, who smiled to acknowledge my presence. She gave me a quick motherly squeeze on my forearm.

"Plutarch." Anna was one of the most educated women at court and she had imparted her love of history to her son. While my husband preferred reading the history of warfare, his mother preferred the philosophers. Her taste in reading material made it much easier for me to talk to her.

"How many times have you read it?'"

She shrugged, "Not enough. I get more out of it each time I read it. You look uncomfortable."

I shifted in my chair and tried to find a way to sit without pressing against the nerves of my back. I was carrying my twelfth child, proof that my marriage had been a fruitful one. Our children provided the Guise family with plenty of sons and daughters to marry across France. Five of our children lay buried in the family crypt back in Joinville, close to the eastern border of France. Losing a child was a common event, but the loss of each one was agony for me. After carrying a being dependent upon me for almost a year and caring for it after its birth, the sudden loss was excruciating. I never got used to the threat of losing a baby, no woman ever did.

Of our healthy children, most were sent to the nursery, where my husband's formidable grandmother had raised generations of children, both Guise and noble families who entrusted their daughters in Antoinette de Bourbon's capable hands. A year ago, the aged Antoinette died, which meant that my youngest, Renee, lived with us at the Hotel de Guise. I was thrilled my daughter was with me in Paris and hardly missed an opportunity to tend to her myself.

"I understand that my daughter is off making mischief again." Her sharp eyes missed nothing. It was not my place to shield Catherine of Lorraine from her own mother; if Anna planned on upbraiding her for her actions, that was her prerogative. Still, I did not want to implicate myself and put myself in an awkward position with my influential mother-in-law.

"She's still dealing with Louis' estate. She's cleaning out his personal items, finally." That was partly true—the elderly Duc de Montpensier had crammed their home with items and now, Catherine faced the task of dispensing with them. Many items were packed off to the far corners of France to her step-children as part of their inheritance. Others were collecting dust until Catherine could find a way to sell them and make a profit. Overall, she was luckier than most of us—her husband had left her quite a fortune and she at least was not faced with paying off the taxes from her father's death over a decade ago. That duty fell to his heir, a burden Henri had faced when his own father died suddenly in 1563.

"I doubt that everything in that house qualifies as a priceless antique. Some of those items might bring another kind of price, no?" She continued to scan my face and I squirmed.

"This child will not get off of my back!" I cried out loudly enough that the entire room could hear me, hoping to change the subject. The matrons in the Queen Mother's entourage gave me tight smiles of sympathy. Anyone who had carried a child before knew the daily discomforts that came with the condition. Beside me, Anna snorted, but chose to let the subject drop.

About the Author
Laura du Pre is an emerging author of historical fiction. This is Laura's second book and the second in the Three Graces Trilogy.

Laura holds a Master's Degree in History from Middle Tennessee State University. Before writing full time she worked as an archivist, records manager, and a contributor for historical publications. She lives in the Deep South with her cranky elderly cat, Owen.

You can download a FREE copy of the Three Graces short story *Safe in my Arms* at her website, www.lauradupre.com.

Also by Laura du Pre
The Three Graces Trilogy

Almost a Queen

Lady of the Court

Fate's Mistress

The French Mistresses Trilogy (Winter 2017-2018)

The Valois Mistress

The Uncrowned Queen

The Queen's Nemesis

Copyright
Copyright © 2017 by Laura du Pre